AF191974

Lina Fischer

The Falling of the Stars

novum pro

www.novum-publishing.co.uk

© 2022 novum publishing

ISBN 978-3-99131-101-0
Editing: Ashleigh Brassfield, DipEdit
Cover photos: Paultarasenko, Alinamd | Dreamstime.com
Cover design, layout & typesetting: novum publishing

www.novum-publishing.co.uk

To those who inspired it

and will not read it

The Falling of the Stars

"Who are you?" they asked.

"A demon to some, angel to others," I responded. "But you could also just call me your queen."

Nothing would be the same after tonight. He swore he would come back for me, and I was ready to destroy him. *He took everything from me, and I am ready to do the same. I overcame everything he has thrown at me and came back stronger.* I walked down the marble stairs, thinking of every loss I had suffered, and I could feel the power surrounding me.

Prologue

I was always the girl who stole the spotlight; no matter who they were, people would always look up to me. I'm not going to lie, it's an exhausting job to do, especially when everybody has such high expectations.

After I was orphaned, the king and queen adopted me because the queen wasn't able to have children of her own. They are the best parents I could have asked for, and I'm so grateful for them. There are downsides to it, though; I don't have many friends, because my parents are scared that someone would hurt me. I don't know why they are so afraid; why would anybody want to hurt me? At least I have my best friend, Eden; he came to us after both his parents died in the war against Aaron, whoever that is.

We were babies when my parents took him in, it was a big scandal when Eden's father was killed in the war and I feel connected to him because of everything we've had to go through together. We share the spotlight; after all, we're the future of our people, since everybody expects us to marry each other.

I woke up to three gentle knocks on my door, as always. I opened the door for Eden.

He looked especially beautiful this morning. His soft brown hair looked almost gold as the sunlight consumed the room. "Hey you," he said.

"You know, you knocking at my door every morning gets annoying," I said, still half asleep.

"And you know that I like to annoy you."

I chuckled. *Typical Eden.* "What's on the agenda for today, my knight?" I asked him.

"Don't tell me you forgot? Everybody is preparing for your birthday ball!" he exclaimed hastily.

"I knew I forgot something! Well, let me get dressed and I'll meet you downstairs in a second," I told him before closing the door.

I dressed myself in a skirt, a lace top, and a white cardigan. As I walked downstairs, I saw some of the staff busy preparing for the ball. I couldn't help but feel bad that they had so much to do because of me.

In the large, high-ceilinged dining room, the table was ready, and I noticed that I was the last to arrive for breakfast. I took my place next to Eden and saw that Dad looked more tense than usual.

"Hey Dad, everything alright?" I asked.

"Good morning sweetheart – everything's fine, I'm just a little bit stressed about the preparations for the ball," he said, continuing to read the national newspaper.

"Dad, please stop worrying about it, you know that I'll love whatever you do!"

"Of course, honey, I know that, but after all it is your eighteenth birthday, and that is something that only happens once in a lifetime."

"I know, but I also know that I'll never be able to forget the night either way."

Mom was taken aback for a moment. "What do you mean?"

"I don't know, I just have the feeling that this night will change everything," I said excitedly.

"I, for one, think that it'll be great, and I can't wait to see what you've got planned." Eden had a spark in his eyes.

I didn't really feel like celebrating my birthday. *It shouldn't be such a big deal, I don't even like birthdays. Everybody knows that whenever we celebrate my birthday, something unfortunate happens. Last year, Eden got food poisoning along with everyone else. The year before we had a huge storm come over Ilimara. However, if I keep being optimistic, it might just be the best birthday I will ever have.* I spent the rest of the day helping with the preparations and it lifted my spirits. I couldn't wait to see the end product. The days went by in a flurry of activity, and all of a sudden the day was here.

The Greenhouse

Just before midnight came three gentle knocks on my door. I jumped out of my bed and felt my stomach tingle as I opened the door. Eden took my hand and led me into our humid greenhouse at the end of the palace.

It was my favourite place in the palace and he knew that. The light shimmering through the glass made his eyes look even bluer; his gaze made me feel like a thousand butterflies were bursting into life in my stomach. As the tower clock rang midnight, he took something from behind his back.

"Happy Birthday, my star," he said as I opened the gift.

It was a bracelet, a chain of stars, and it was stunning.

"Eden, it's beautiful, thank you so much!" I exclaimed joyfully.

"Thank *you* for never leaving my side. I don't know what I'd do without you," he said, and I could've sworn I saw his eyes glisten.

"I could never leave you, you're my best friend and I care about you," I said with tears in my eyes. I looked up at the sky and saw multiple shooting stars flash past. "Wow, Eden, its magical," I said quietly.

"You're my best friend after all, you deserve only the best," he whispered in my ear.

"Yes, best friends, that's what we are."

I wanted to memorise every feature of his face, but he stopped me, putting his hand on my cheek. He leaned in and his soft lips met mine. He smelled like cinnamon. A lifetime of happiness bloomed in my chest, only to be replaced with pain as though it had been pierced with a sharp blade.

"Eden…" I took a deep breath. "You know we can't do that, not after last time," I whispered.

"Astoria, you can hurt me, I won't blame you if you do, but please give us a chance," he begged.

"I wish I could, Eden, I really wish I could do that, but I just can't."

I slowly started to distance myself from him and the situation as he held me back and looked me in the eyes. "Astoria..." was the last thing I heard as I rushed away from the greenhouse back to my room and fell into my warm, soft bed.

Memories From the Past

I opened my eyes, confused at first about the wet pillow pressed against my cheek. The events of last night came flooding back as I woke up fully, and I laid on my back looking up at the window above my bed. It was almost starting to freeze because of the cold air outside.

When I was a little girl and winter came, I would dress up as the northern queen and Mom would braid my hair. Dad would teach me how to dance and never lose hope, even as I bruised his toes.

I would run to Eden's room and let him try the cookies we baked, and he would always tell me that they were delicious – even if his face said something very different.

Life was easy, uncomplicated.

This year was different. Everything changed after the night in July when Eden had asked me to be with him. Of course, I said yes; that's what everybody expected of me. Eden should have known that I had to say yes, even if that wasn't how I felt in that moment.

I told my parents that I'm just not ready to commit yet, but I am ready; just not with him.

I love him more than anything in the world, and I can't risk our friendship like that, it means the world to me.

A knock on my door pulled me out of my thoughts. I had no energy left so I just said, "Come on in," quickly putting on a smile, and then said "Good morning."

"Good morning birthday princess!" Mom said brightly. I flinched at the noise, and she noticed that something wasn't right. "Astoria, what's bothering you?" she asked, worried.

"It's Eden," I sighed, "he just doesn't understand that I am not ready to be with him, and I don't want to lose him."

"Oh darling, I'm so sorry, please don't feel like you have to do something that you don't want to. I'm sure Eden understands that, right?"

"Yes, he does, but he's constantly trying to convince me and it puts so much pressure on me, but I'm doing it for our sake, so we won't ruin our friendship."

I put my heavy head onto the pillow, and I could still feel the tears from last night.

"Do you love him, Astoria?" she asked seriously.

"Of course, with all my heart, Mom," I said into my pillow.

"Then tell him," she said.

"I don't think he'd understand. I'll just try to avoid him as much as possible," I said.

"That's not how you handle situations, and you know that. That's not how I raised you," she said sternly.

"I know, but just give me some time to figure out what I should do next," I said pleadingly.

"Do what you think is right, I trust you. Now, let me braid your hair," she said, tugging at the ends of my hair. We sat there in comfortable silence until she cleared her throat.

"You know, Astoria, nobody is expecting you to marry Eden or be with him. It's your own decision, we won't force you to do anything," she assured me.

"But you would be happy and proud, wouldn't you?" I said, frustrated.

"Yes, but we are going to be as happy and proud of you either way, it's your life and you should spend it with someone who you truly love," she said.

"Thank you Mom, I love you." I leaned back and giving her a hug.

When she finished braiding my hair, she put a diamond-encrusted tiara on my head to match my big, magical braid.

"I wore this when I met your father on his birthday. I thought it would fit the occasion perfectly," she said, correcting its position.

"It's beautiful, thank you so much!" I said, admiring its beauty.

"Now go dress yourself, the ball starts soon. Your dress is in the closet down the hall," she said before leaving my room.

I looked at my reflection in the mirror and my once green eyes seemed to turn into the colour of the stars. When I looked closer, they were green again.

That was interesting. I've never experienced something like that before, but I'm probably just imagining things.

I decided to make my way down the hall to get my dress, and as soon as I stepped out of my room, I heard footsteps approaching me. I instantly knew who it was, and I tried to walk as fast as possible in the hopes that I could hide somewhere.

"Astoria!" I heard him call. I tried walking faster but soon felt a hand grabbing my wrist.

"Let me go!" I exclaimed.

"Stop running away from me. Do you really think you can avoid me?" he laughed.

"Eden, let me go, now!" I said impatiently. "Stop it, dammit." I bit back tears as he grabbed my wrists and pulled them towards his chest.

"I'll never stop. You are a coward, and you know it. You and I both are. Stop lying to yourself!" he exclaimed.

"I don't care about you!" The bitter lie flew from my lips as I desperately tried to pull away from him.

A hurt expression crossed his eyes for a brief second before impassiveness took over. He let me go. He shook his head, staring at me as if he could see into the depths of my very soul. "Such a goddamned liar," he said, turning his back and walking away.

I knew that the very thing I feared the most just happened: I lost him.

I shook my head and walked the familiar hallway all the way to the end. I stepped into the big room full of gowns and suits and made my way to my section.

There, laid out, was the most alluring gown I'd ever laid my eyes on. The light blue shimmered with its diamonds and the giant skirt was the perfect size to get a little bit of space, but just roomy enough to be able to dance the night away. I struggled to get the zipper up, but after some time I succeeded.

Green eyes looked back at me as I fixed my mascara in the mirror after the argument, and stepped into the hallway once again.

The Truth

As I descended the grand staircase into the ballroom, I heard classical music playing. The marble stairs were decorated with candles and the atmosphere was something I'd never experienced before. Candles and chandeliers lit the room with a comfortable shimmer.

When I came back to reality, I noticed that it was quiet, and all eyes were on me. I smiled graciously and saw that Eden stood at the end of the stairs holding out his arm. I couldn't deny him in front of every noble in the kingdom, but of course, that was the point. I put on my dearest smile and kissed his cheek as I took his arm. I got a warm welcome from everyone and finally they started dancing.

"I don't want to ruin your birthday, Astoria, so let's at least put our differences aside for a moment and enjoy ourselves," Eden said, not quite meeting my eyes. He held his hand out with a questioning look.

It took me a moment, but finally I took his hand and he led me onto the dance floor. A new song had just started, and we danced like we had since we were children, his hand on my waist and mine behind his neck.

I wasn't able to look him in the eyes after what had happened; there are some things you can't put aside, after all. He lifted my chin, forcing me to meet his eyes, and I wasn't sure what to expect.

"Please look at me, Astoria. I'm sorry for how I behaved, it's just that I'm done waiting for someone that maybe doesn't even want me," he said quietly.

"Eden, I love you more than anything, but you just saw what happens if we don't stop that right now. We can't work, as much as we want it to, it won't," I said, talking into his chest.

"I know, but it'll take me some time to process this. I don't think we should see each other until then," he mumbled, and with that the song ended and he left me stunned.

As I made my way over to the bar, I suddenly felt someone bump into me. I almost fell, but the stranger caught me with his hands on my waist. I looked up into grey eyes, staring at me.

"I'm sorry for bumping into you, are you alright?" I asked the handsome stranger.

"You were quite lucky, that fall could've torn your dress easily," he smirked.

His ginger hair shone in the light from the chandelier, and I couldn't get past the thought that I must have seen him before; there was an instant connection.

"Do I know you by any chance?"

"We'll meet again soon, Astoria," he said before disappearing into the shadows.

The Last Dance

I made my way up to my mother, who stood across the room talking to some of the guests. I greeted some of them on my way over and she put her arm around me.

"Astoria, let me introduce you to Mr. and Mrs. Fray," she said joyfully.

"Darling, let me tell you, you look remarkable in this dress!" Mrs. Fray exclaimed.

"Oh, thank you so much, and thank you for coming!" I told them.

"They lead a very successful academy in the north," Mom explained.

"Wow, I always wished to attend an academy, but I just never had the opportunity," I said wistfully.

"Well, from what I've heard you would be a great student at our academy, and it would be our pleasure to welcome you," Mr. Fray said.

I blinked. *Did I really just get an opportunity to do what I want most?*

"I think we'll have to talk about that first," Mom exclaimed with a sweet smile that didn't reach her eyes, and I knew that it was a lost cause.

"It was a pleasure meeting you, Mr. and Mrs. Fray," I said as I shook their hands.

I took my mother's hand and lead her onto the dance floor.

"No, Astoria, please, you know I don't like to dance!" she said, blushing.

"Mom, come on, please, it's my 18th Birthday!" I exclaimed happily.

She took my hand and we started to dance to an upbeat song. "I remember dancing with you when you were a little girl. You would always step on my shoes and get them dirty, so I would have to take them off," she said, raising her voice a little over the loud music. She was beaming with happiness. *I can't remember seeing her as happy as she is right now.*

"You only let me stand on your shoes because I wasn't able to walk!" I protested. She chuckled and we danced happily, singing along with our whole hearts like we used to do when I was little.

Eventually she said she had to check on her makeup, and with that she disappeared.

I went to get some of the delicious appetisers, that was the best part about these balls after all.

The First Encounter

A high, familiar scream pierced the air. I searched for a familiar face in the crowd as the guests jostled to get out of the ballroom.

I spotted Eden in a corner, talking heatedly with my Dad, and I knew that something bad must've happened. I searched for Mom in the crowd, which seemed to get less crowded with every second that passed.

"Where's Mom?" I screamed at the top of my lungs, and the two of them quickly schooled their expressions.

"Astoria, everything is fine, Mom is safe, don't worry," Dad said, but I knew better. I saw the look on Eden's face, and there's nothing that could've convinced me they were telling the truth.

"Don't lie to me on my own birthday, I know damn well that nothing is fine! Where is Mom? Where is she?" My eyes began to burn, and I felt tears falling down my cheeks. I knew that Dad wouldn't tell me the truth, so I turned to Eden and asked once again where Mom was.

"Astoria, it's too late, there's nothing we can do for her. The only thing you can do to help is to come with me right now," he demanded.

"What do you mean it's too late, too late for what, Eden?" More tears flooded down my face, and my vision started to go blurry. *What is happening? Why won't they tell me the truth?*

"Eden, please answer me!" I said quietly. I saw that it hurt him to stay quiet; his eyes were set firmly away from mine.

I noticed that the room was empty and there was no one else but us inside. The only thing I heard was my own heartbeat, racing faster every second.

"Tell me where she is right now!" I yelled at them.

"Astoria come with us, it is too dangerous for you to be out here!" Dad demanded.

"I won't come with you if you don't tell me where she is right now!" I raised my voice so it echoed in the grand ballroom, and when I didn't get a response I ran.

I ran as fast as I could, and soon I was too far gone to hear whatever Eden screamed. I ran and searched for anything that could help me find her. My gown was too long to run in, so I tore it apart, barely covering my knees now. I ran until I couldn't breathe, so confused, trying to process what was happening.

In that moment I heard the loud scream again. This time it sounded even more pained, and I knew why the voice sounded so familiar. It was Mom.

I tried to find the direction it came from and fixed my hair as I started to run towards the throne room. Passing a mirror, I saw that my mascara was all over my face, my hair was a mess, and the once beautiful gown was destroyed.

I ran and heard more and more screams and pushed the door open to find something that would haunt me to the end of my days. My eyes searched the familiar room that I had spent so many days in crying from laughter.

I spotted Mom in the middle of the room, struggling against someone I had never seen before. "Mom!" I screamed, and I felt the tension ease as I saw that she was still alive.

From the unknown figure came a voice as dark as night. "What a delight, seeing the guest of honour after all this time!"

"Leave her alone, you monster!" Mom yelled, and I immediately knew that this wouldn't end well.

"Who are you?" I asked the figure, and as he turned, I saw his face for the first time.

"Oh dear, don't tell me you haven't heard of me. I am the most powerful of them all!"

"Why are you here, what do you want?" I asked angrily.

"I want you, and the power that you hold."

"What are you talking about? What power?"

He seemed to enjoy this far more than he should. "Amaris, don't tell me that you've kept that secret from your little girl all this time?" he said, amused.

"It is too dangerous for her to know what she's capable of…" Mom said, so quietly that I could barely understand her.

"Mom, what are you talking about, what kind of power?"

"Yes, Amaris, tell her," the figure said sarcastically.

"I can't, I'm sorry sweetie, I am so sorry for everything," she said, her eyes glistening.

"Well then, let's see if you live up to expectations, my child."

With that, my mother flew across the room and collided with the cold wall with a sickening thud.

"Mom!" I cried, and rushed to her side. "What did you do to her, you monster?" I screamed, but before I could say anything else I was hit with a foreboding orb that crept up my body and stopped right before it reached my heart.

"My dear, show me what you got, I don't waste my time at boring balls." He waved his hand through the room, and I felt a breeze against my soft skin. "Show me now, or your mother won't live another second," he said calmly.

I couldn't speak, fighting the urge to run up to him and attack him.

"As you please, my child," and he shot another ball at her. Anger burned in my chest as I saw her chest go still.

He started to approach her, and I was driven with more fury with every step he took. I felt a strange power surrounding me, but I didn't have time to think about it.

I almost flew at him. "Leave her alone, you sick monster!" I screamed, so loud I thought the windows would shatter.

"Don't be so hasty girl, I just want to make sure I got her," he said, grinning.

"You," I said, as I took a step towards him, "you killed my mother!"

The power was almost consuming me. I had never felt as powerful as I did in that moment. "Go to hell!" was the only thing I was able to yell before the power unleashed and consumed the whole room.

He was hurt, but not as badly as I hoped, and the only thing he said before vanishing into the dark was:

"Do not worry my child, I will be back."

The Aftershock

I jumped as I heard footsteps approaching, and felt an instant relief as I saw Eden's face light up.

"Astoria!" he yelled as he ran towards me. "I heard you scream, is everything alright?" he asked, worried. Suddenly, the sharp pain came back, and with every breath I took it consumed more and more of my body.

I looked over Eden's shoulder at my mother. *She's dead because of me.* I broke down in his arms.

"She's dead, she's gone," I heard my father say as he checked her pulse. I saw a tear roll down his face as I walked over to him. He put his arms around Mom and me, and it was like time stopped. The memories flashed before my eyes like a nightmare. *This will haunt me until the last breath I take.*

"Dad, I'm sorry," I said quietly, but he shushed me before I could say anything more.

"Astoria, none of this is your fault. We knew it was only a matter of time until he came for you," he tried to reassure me.

"Who is he and why is he after me? What did I do to him?" I exclaimed.

"He's the one we do not talk about. He is the devil, one of the most powerful shadows there are. No lighter has ever been able to fight him," he explained.

"What are you talking about?"

"Once there lived shadows and lighters together in peace, demons and angels like you've read about. They got along well and even started their own families – that is until the demons got jealous because the angels had healing power and were able to perform magic. They don't know why; it is said it was a gift from God, because they're his children.

One day a demon went to Satan and begged him to give them a gift, so they could be treated equally. Satan was never one to do as he was told, so he gave him a task to complete first: He would only give them power if they sacrificed every angel they knew and brought them to him.

The demons did as they were told. They came back to the village and attacked the angels. They weren't ready, got taken by surprise, and had no chance against them. But the demons didn't manage to capture everyone; seven of them managed to escape."

"The seven archangels, right?" I interrupted.

"Yes, the seven archangels Michael, Gabriel, Uriel, Raphael, Saraqael, Raquel, and Remiel managed to escape the shadows and searched for protection from God.

God was furious when he heard the news, and he cast a spell to prevent the shadows from entering our world. Nonetheless, some of them always found their way through with portals, and a war started between the lighters and shadows.

It went on for over a decade, and many people died. Everyone thinks that all of this is a silly myth, but we know it is the truth," he told me.

"How do we know it isn't a myth?"

"Because they still exist."

Clarity

"What do you mean they still exist?»

"Don't you understand? Why he came to get you? Why you were able to scare him off?"

"But how?" I was getting more and more confused.

"You have special powers. You are not ordinary," he said with proud eyes.

"Dad what are you implying?" I asked, trying to get everything sorted out in my head.

"Tell me, Astoria, have you noticed anything strange in the last few days?" he questioned.

I remembered the headaches I had, the strange feeling in my chest and the change of colour in my eyes. "Yes, I have," I answered.

"Now tell me, what colour did your eyes change to?" he asked.

I only remembered snippets of the moment that I noticed the change. The only thing I saw was my eyes having the same colour of the night sky with stars.

"They were like the night sky, with sparkles like stars," I answered him. His eyebrows shot up.

I saw him looking over at Eden, remembering that he was in the room as well. They exchanged a glance, and I could tell that Dad had given him a signal.

"Dad, what does that mean?" I asked.

"Don't worry honey, you're safe here. Please go rest in your room, I'm sure you have much to process," and with that said, he left the room after Eden.

I wasn't ready to leave my mother and I took her hand in mine and just sat there for a few minutes trying to find a real explanation for what just had happened.

"Mom, I wish you were here. I feel so alone. I wish you would've told me the truth; that's what I deserved as your daughter. Why did you lie to me?" I whispered into her cold hair as the tears came streaming down my face as I got more and more frustrated.

I stayed next to her until morning came, and with it people to move her. I took one last glance at the woman who raised me.

On the way to my room, I came across some portraits of my mother and me. It had been our tradition to take a picture on my birthday every year. Suddenly a memory came flooding back:

"Astoria! Hurry up, before we take the photo I'd like to give you something," she said joyfully, handing me a beautiful necklace with a star on it.

"Mom, it's absolutely breath-taking, where did you get it?" I asked as I put the necklace on.

"Let's say it belonged to a very special person that wanted me to give you this on your sixteenth birthday," she said.

"Well, tell that person that I absolutely love this necklace and I will never take it off," I said happily.

"Now ladies, are you ready for your big photoshoot?" the photographer asked with a big smile on his face.

"Yes, we are," we both said, and laughed.

"Now say Happy Birthday Astoria!" he exclaimed as he took a photo.

The flash brought me back to reality as I realised that I instinctively held onto my necklace, which felt cold against my skin.

I heard footsteps approaching and saw that Eden was walking towards me. "Did you know?" I asked him, furious.

"What do you mean?" he said with a questioning look on his face.

"Did you know that I'm a lighter?" I exclaimed.

"I am sorry Astor–"

"So you knew the whole time and you never told me?" I interrupted him angrily.

"I wasn't allowed to, it was for your own safety," he said.

"Well look where that got us! I just can't believe you lied to my face like that for so long," I said, shaking my head. I felt the exhaustion in my eyes as I looked at the person I once knew best. "I feel like I don't know who you are anymore. Why are you always on their side and never on mine?"

"I care about you, that's why, and because I know what risks come with knowing the truth!"

I felt like I was on the edge of discovering another secret. "Eden...are you a lighter as well?" I asked him, intrigued.

He sighed. "Yes, I am, and that's why we're going to the academy in the north; they'll teach you how to use your power and everything you need to know about it."

"When do we leave?" I asked.

"Right now, the staff already packed everything you need, come on." He dragged me to the giant front door which led to the palace garden.

I shivered at the cold breeze on my skin and wished I had my cardigan with me. Lost in thought, I laid my eyes on the car that was waiting at the front gate.

We made our way through the garden that I had spent so many afternoons reading books in, and soon we came to a stop as we arrived at the front gate.

I saw Dad talking with the driver and mentally prepared to say goodbye to him.

"Astoria, never forget, I love you more than anything, and you can always come back if you want to," he said as he hugged me tight.

"I love you too Dad, may we meet again."

He took a step back and opened the door for me.

I stepped into the car and Eden joined me soon after. The chauffeur started driving as I tried to get my head around everything that happened.

Not soon after we left our kingdom, with so many questions left unanswered.

Nightmares

As Mom came down the stairs, I knew that something was off. "Mom, is everything alright?" I asked as she walked past me.

"No, honey, but I can't tell you what's going on. Please go find your Dad," she said, brushing past me.

"Mom, stop, please talk to me, I can help you," I begged as I hurried after her.

"No, Astoria, it's for your own safety. I love you darling, may we meet again," she said, and disappeared behind the door.

What is going on? Why was she so serious? Confused, I just stood there looking after her. As I decided to go look for Dad, I heard cruel screams and my head shot up.

Mom was hanging from the chandelier right next to me and was about to suffocate.

"Mom!" I screamed. I tried to help her, but my hands trembled and I started hyperventilating.

What should I do? What should I do? My panic was building. I couldn't move, I couldn't scream; I could only stare at my mother as the life was sucked out of her.

I watched with fear as I desperately tried to move once again.

"Mom," I tried to scream, but nothing came out of my mouth.

No, this can't be happening, I can't just watch my mother die without doing something! I felt helpless as the colour slowly drained from her skin; it was as if I was paralysed.

I cried and buried my face in my palms as I saw her taking her last breath. *No, no, no, this isn't happening, this can't be happening, not my mother, anyone but my mother.*

"Astoria," I heard someone scream, "Astoria, wake up!" Slowly I realised that I was in the car with Eden. "Astoria, you're drenched in sweat, what happened?" he asked.

I felt more tired than ever as the panic gripping my chest eased. "It was nothing, I just had a nightmare," I said to him.

I could've helped her, I could've saved her that night, they all feel sorry for me but it's my fault, all my fault. The terrible hole that she left in my heart ached miserably.

"Alright, if you say so. I hope you're ready to impress, because we're almost there." Eden smiled, and I calmed down some more.

I had to distract myself from the truth. Staring at the academy, my biggest dream for so long, I still felt a spark of excitement despite the harrowing events that led up to it coming true.

I looked out the window and saw busy streets that reminded me of our capital, back in Ilimara; the narrow streets with little shops and the river flowing through the city. It was breath-taking. As we drove through the streets I laid my eyes upon a vast cathedral that looked like it was still in the 1800s with it's grand door and details.

Soon after, we arrived at the academy, and I was stunned by the stately building before us. It was very similar to the cathedral I had seen earlier, but it was very welcoming. It reminded me of our palace at home, just way bigger. *That will be my new home for I don't know how long.* I was starting to get cold feet, thinking about how many students there must be and that I was new and nobody knew me. *Well, that's the problem, everybody knows me.*

I didn't know anything about them and the world that they live in, their powers, their history... suddenly I felt overwhelmed.

"Alright, Princess Astoria, are you ready for your new adventure?" Eden held out a hand and helped me out of the car.

I took one more look at the huge building before taking Eden's hand and disappearing through the front door.

The New Chapter

As I took the first step into the building that I would now call my home, I stared at the room around me. The light was soft, a staircase led to god knows where, and the portraits on the walls gave me the impression of a secret society. The hallway ran the length of the building and ended with a large door, which led into the dining hall, as I could have guessed.

It was as gorgeous as it was from the outside and I couldn't hide my amazement. I heard Eden chuckle next to me as I stared at every single detail.

"It's amazing," I said, mouth agape.

"You'll get used to it after a while," he said, looking at the portraits with a mysterious look in his eye.

"Have you been here before?" I asked him, looking into his eyes, shimmering in the low light.

"Yes. Do you remember when I suddenly left and you didn't knew where I was?"

Of course I remember, how could I forget.

I woke up one day looking forward to spending time with Eden. When I went to his room and knocked, the maid told me that he had left the night before. I will never forget the look on the her face.

I was devastated, not only because he left without saying good-bye, but also because we kissed the night before and he had told me that he loved me. I slowly recovered, but it took me months to get over it.

I had no clue that my parents made him go to the academy. I thought he left because he didn't mean what he said the night before.

"Eden, I didn't know that they made you go. I thought you left because you didn't love me," I said hastily, afraid that he would hear the vulnerability in my voice.

"I did love you, and I tried everything to get them to let me stay, but they said it was for the best. It was, I learned more than I ever could've back home," he told me, and I knew he was right; as much as it hurt me, it was the best for him.

"I knew something must have happened. You weren't the same when you came home; you were so distant and you would avoid me as much as possible. I thought you hated me and I couldn't wrap my head around why," I exclaimed, remembering the time where I was so desperately in need of a best friend who was never around.

"I knew you were a lighter as well, and that you are more special than all of us. I thought if I stayed away from you I could protect you better and I wouldn't have to lie to you all the time. Believe me, it broke me knowing that I knew more of you than you knew yourself," he said with a sad expression on his face.

"I hope I'm not interrupting," I heard a familiar voice say, "but I'd like to welcome you to the academy, Astoria."

"Mrs. Fray! Lovely meeting you, I had hoped to see you again, what a nice welcome!" I exclaimed as she welcomed me with a warm hug.

"Welcome back Eden, it's a delight having you around as always," she said, holding out her hand. "Now, Astoria, how do you like the academy so far?"

"Mrs. Fray, may I say you have a gorgeous academy? I am at a loss for words, thank you for having me," I said with a smile.

"Oh, dear, we are more than happy to have you! We've heard that you were taken by surprise as you discovered your power – I'm a little bit surprised that it took you that long to realise," she said with a warm smile.

"Yes, it was certainly a surprise, especially because everyone knew except for me." The cold undertone in my voice reflected the betrayal that I felt that night.

"And let me say I am so sorry for your loss, may the queen rest in peace. At least she passed away in her sleep and didn't feel any pain," she told us with a sympathetic look.

What was she talking about? Did she not know the truth about how Mom died? Why were they lying to everyone about it?

Eden saw that I was confused and shot me a silencing look.

Mrs. Fray noticed my confusion, but fortunately she misunderstood. "I am sorry if I have offended you in any way," she said, looking concerned.

"Don't worry Mrs. Fray, everything is alright. It seems as if the gathering is about to start, should we head in?" Eden asked me.

"I'm ready whenever you are." And with that we stepped into a gigantic room full of people.

The crowd was a tumult of voices until I heard Mr. Fray clear his throat.

"Hello students, and welcome to this gathering. Today we come together to welcome a new student in our academy, Astoria," he said, pointing in my direction. "It's an honour having you here! She's new to all of this and it would mean the world to us if you would help her out a little bit. As for the rest of you, I am happy to announce that the final exams are officially over! Congratulations everyone, now go and enjoy the rest of your evening."

With that, students started to leave the room and go back to their dorms.

Some people had stayed in the room, and I was getting uncomfortable as I noticed that they were all watching me. *What did I expect? That I could just walk in here and everyone would like me?*

I saw three boys making their way up to us and expected them to come up to me, but instead they hugged Eden and said hello to him.

"Eden, how have you been brother? It's nice having you back!" a young man with blond hair said. His eyes reminded me of the ocean, and I realised that I was staring at him.

"This is Astoria everyone, we grew up together and she's new here," Eden said, introducing me to his friends.

"Hi, nice to meet you Astoria. I'm Ash and these are the dorks I call my friends," the blond man said with a genuine smile. "Nice to meet you Ash. Hello everyone," I said, and finally took a good look at them.

32

Most of them were average looking boys, the ones that you'd expect to be here, but one in particular caught my eye. I would recognise his grey eyes anywhere, as well as his ginger hair, perfectly parted in the middle, making his hair fall to each side.

"You're the one I bumped into at the ball! What a coincidence meeting you here," I said happily. I had found the stranger once again, just as he said I would.

I heard the others whisper and couldn't get past the feeling that I must have said something wrong.

"I don't know what you're talking about, I've never seen you in my entire life," he said, uninterested and cold.

I'm not sensitive, but that hurt my feelings, especially because he made me look like an idiot. "No, I'm sure it was you," I said, sticking to my guns.

"What's she talking about, Nathaniel?" Ash asked.

"I have no clue. Now, if you'll excuse me, I have other places to be," he said, and I stared after him as he left the room.

Why didn't he just tell them the truth, why would he be ashamed? While I was talking to some of the boys, I heard Eden's phone ring. He answered the call, but the only thing I could make out before he left the room was that it had something to do with politics back home. *Great, now I'm alone with boys I've known for less than 20 minutes.*

Ash came up to me and greeted me with a smile. "So, Astoria, what brought you here?"

"Funny story. There are some things you have to know before I start..." I told him the story of how I discovered my powers, though of course I left out the part where my mother died.

He listened without interrupting me, and it was good being able to talk to someone who wasn't involved in the whole situation.

"Wow, I'm sure that was a lot, especially meeting Aaron when you first discover your powers. You must have been so afraid, how did you manage to survive?" he asked carefully.

"I didn't know who he was, I'd never heard of him, and when he attacked me I didn't even think, it just happened. Everything happened so fast." I said, remembering that moment once again. "Why are you here Ash, what's your story?"

"Well, I can't remember a time where I wasn't here at the academy. My parents sent me here when I was little and I never felt like going back home, you know – I don't get along with them really, so I decided that I'm better off here," he said.

"I'm sorry, I'm sure that's not easy for you. I never knew my real parents," I told him.

"Wait, so the king and queen aren't your real parents?"

"No, they adopted me when I was a baby. I never got to know my birth parents." The thought that they just left me there on the front porch always saddened me.

"At least you have a beautiful family now, that's all that counts," he said, trying to be comforting. "Hey man, everything alright?"

I turned around to see Eden hastily making his way over to us. "I'm sorry but I have to return, they have problems back home and you know how your Dad can be. I'll come back as soon as I get the chance, I'm sorry, Ash will look after you," he said while picking up his things, and gave me a kiss on my forehead. "May we meet again," he said before taking off. Before I could process what happened he was gone, leaving me and Ash alone.

Your New Enemy

After Eden's departure I felt alone and helpless, so I decided to stay in the gathering room and just have a look around. It was a mysterious room with the light so low, and a smell like old books on a winter evening. I made my way around and came across a bookshelf. I took a book out without thinking and opened it on a random page. It was a drawing which I felt like I had seen before, on my way here.

It felt familiar when I looked at it, an angel falling from the sky with a baby in his arms and a demon looking down at them from hell. It was interesting how the artist could tell a story with just one drawing. I turned the page, but before I could get a closer look, I heard the door open.

Ash had come back from the bathroom. "So, you're interested in our history?" he asked with an eyebrow raised.

"Can you blame me? This is all new to me, and everyone saying that I'm something special doesn't help me at all." I told him. *And it's true. I'm sick of the fact that nobody ever tells me the truth, so I will investigate myself. At least I can trust myself.*

"Well, good luck with that, but I should show you your dorm, come on." I hesitated to put the book back. *It would help me.* "Are you coming?" Ash called from the other side of the room, and with that I put the book back and made my way out of the room.

As we walked down the hallway, I couldn't help but notice that it was quiet. "Tell me Ash, why is it so quiet when there are so many students here?" I asked him as we walked up the stairs I had seen when I first entered the academy.

"Normally it's not this quiet, but today is special – the final exams are over, so everyone's celebrating in the ball room."

"Ash, please don't tell me I'm the reason you're not going? By all means, get out of my sight and go enjoy," I assured him.

"Let me show you your room, it's not like the party's ending anytime soon anyway," he insisted. As we started up another set of stairs I was lost in thought, trying to memorise everything. "So, what's the deal with you and Nathaniel?" I heard him ask.

"To be honest, there is no deal. We met at my birthday ball a while ago because I bumped into him," I answered, knowing that wasn't the whole truth. *He did know me back then.*

"No, you must be joking, Nathaniel would never step a foot into a royal castle," he explained.

I was starting to feel like an idiot again, so I changed the subject, but I couldn't get what Ash said out of my head. *Why would Nathaniel attend the ball if he would never go into a castle? What was his deal?*

I realised that we stopped in front of a door which was at the very end of the corridor. "Well then, I'm sure they brought up your luggage. I'll see you tomorrow for breakfast, and if you have a problem, you know where to find me," he said with a smile before disappearing.

I opened the handcrafted door and the smell of hot tea welcomed me in, as well as a woman sitting at the desk. I closed the door behind me and wasn't sure what I should do. *Who is she, and what's she doing here?*

She turned around and her eyes lit up as she saw me. "Hey, you must be Astoria, right?" she asked me with a lovely, light voice.

"Yes, I am. May I ask what you are doing in my dorm?"

"I'm your roommate, duh! I've been dying to finally get to know you," she said as she stood up and gave me a hug. "I'm sorry, but I couldn't wait to decorate our room, I hope it's to your liking," she said, pointing around the room.

It was beautiful, like something out of a fairytale; my bed was the one next to the window and you could see the campus from here perfectly. She had decorated her bed with a lot of plants, and some of them were hanging from the ceiling. I felt calmer and more comfortable. *At least I got a nice roommate.* The room was laid out like a regular dorm room, but bigger. The two beds had drawers built into the base for extra storage, which is a genius idea.

There was a desk by a window and in the corner of the room there was a window seat as well. I realised that she had her wall decorated with a mirror and flowers, it looked stunning.

It was then when I realised that we had our own bathroom, which was I was pleased about. I stepped into the well-lit room and saw a sink, a toilet, and a big shower, decorated in a rustic style.

"We have the exact same taste when it comes to decorating, I love it!" I exclaimed with joy. I came back and sat on my bed and realised that I hadn't even asked the stranger for her name. "What's your name by the way?"

"My name is Hera," she answered.

"What's your story, Hera?" I asked the beautiful stranger.

"Well, my parents are Mr. and Mrs. Fray, so I guess that pretty much answers your question. I spent my whole life here and I never really left the city," she told me sadly.

"You have wonderful parents, Hera, I promise you that I will show you my kingdom someday," I assured her.

"That would be great! Enough about me, what's your story?" she asked in return, and so I had to tell my story once again, but of course only the things she needed to know.

"Wow, you met Aaron? That's crazy, he's the most powerful and you managed to scare him off! I guess you really live up to the things they say about you," she said with a smile on her face.

"Great, not even one day here and people are already talking about me." I had hoped to start new without anyone knowing who I am. *I guess that won't work out now.*

Hera chuckled and threw her head back onto her pillow. "Yeah, I'm not trying to scare you, but pretty much everyone knows who you are – they're saying you're special and have special powers, but once again they talk before thinking," she said with a grin on her face.

"I have no idea what they are talking about! I don't know anything about my powers and what they do, so that's where I'm trying to start." I felt hopelessness creeping up on my again.

"I'll help you! Whatever you need, I'll help you with it. I know this place inside and out, don't worry, we will find the truth," she said. We talked for a while and I felt like she really understood me, and it was great to talk to someone who wasn't a boy.

Soon after she fell asleep, and I realised that I forgot my purse in the gathering room, so I decided to make my way to go look for it. I took my light brown cardigan and put it on as I made my way down the corridor. I took the stairs down, but then I had no clue where I was. I tried to find something that I could remember, but it was already late and I was getting tired and cold.

I heard footsteps approaching and I hid behind a corner as I saw someone walk down the hall in a suit. I decided to follow them, but it turned out that the stranger wasn't going where I thought. The halls got darker, and I tried to not make a noise because I knew that this person was hiding something. *God knows what'll happen if he discovers me.* I was glad that I was wearing sneakers and so I followed him into the depths of the academy, always staying a distance behind so he wouldn't notice. I followed him around a corner, but suddenly he wasn't there. Confused, I hurried to the next corner in hopes he would be there, but to no avail.

I looked around and listened out for footsteps, but then I heard a husky voice whispering in my ear, the voice I would never forget. "Why can't you just mind your own goddamn business?" he said angrily. He slammed me against the door and shouted, "Don't follow me, do you understand me? I don't know who you are!"

My wrist started hurting, and I was overwhelmed by what was going on. "You're hurting me," I said angrily, "let me go!"

"Darling, nobody will hear you, we're the only ones here," he said with a smirk.

"What are you hiding, Nathaniel?" I demanded.

"What are you hiding, princess? You killed your own mother! No one could have survived a fight with Aaron," he said, clearly enjoying the look on my face. *How did he know? Nobody's supposed to know what happened that night.* He got under my skin and into my head, and I certainly didn't like that.

"You were there, you liar! Why do you keep saying that you weren't?" I yelled back, and I felt the grip on my wrist tighten.

"Stop that, stop trying to get in my head!" he said, even more angry.

"Then let me go right now!" I screamed as I tried to push him away without success.

"No, you have to learn your lesson, stop following me and mind your own business, do you understand?" he snarled into my ear. The tension grew with every second that passed. I didn't respond. *I won't kneel to any man, especially not Nathaniel. Who does he think he is?* "Answer me!" he screamed. *No way in hell I will obey this man.*

"Well then, as you wish," he said before releasing my wrists, only to cast magic on me. I had no clue what to expect, I didn't even know anything about it, and I was terrified as I saw black dust making its way towards me.

I felt a sharp pain in my chest, and I heard my mother repeatedly say that it was my fault that she's dead. I started crying and hyperventilating remembering the pain I felt when I saw her die in front of my own eyes. It got worse and I heard Nathaniel say, "Stop messing with me. Believe me, it'll only get worse."

I didn't quite catch the next thing he said as I blacked out and fell to the ground.

Inseparable

I woke up with a bad headache and saw that last night left a mark; my wrists were bruised, and they hurt a little bit. I couldn't seem to remember how I ended up here in bed.

The last thing I remembered was Nathaniel saying something to me as I blacked out. *What a douchebag, who does he think he is?* It made me angry how he thought he could get inside my head and manipulate me, but I promised myself it wouldn't work with me.

I wanted to take a shower and wash last night off of me. *I will get my revenge and find out what his deal is with me.* I showered and got dressed. The reflection in the mirror showed a girl who looked perfectly fine and strong, with her hair falling perfectly upon her shoulders.

I decided to put on a skirt and a short blazer which fit perfect together and put on my necklace that my mom gave me. I made my way to the desk to find my things that I had laid out last night.

I heard that Hera was waking up and she murmured something as she stood up and yawned.

"Good morning, are you ok? I was worried when they carried you here last night," she said as she was getting dressed.

"I'm fine, Hera, what happened last night?" I asked her.

"Don't you remember? You blacked out in the corridor, Nathaniel and Ash brought you here last night and said that I should keep an eye on you," she said, confused because I couldn't remember anything.

"He said that? Oh my god, I cannot believe him," I said frustrated as I gave up searching for my bracelet.

"Why, what happened?" she asked again.

"It's a long story and I don't feel like talking right now," I said, trying to change the topic.

"Well then, are you ready so we can head down to eat?" Hera asked as she checked herself out in her mirror.

"I don't feel like eating, but I will keep you company," I said as we left our dorm and made our way to the dining hall.

As I was walking down the corridor a memory came back from last night.

I felt terrible and my chest was hurting, I felt someone carrying me gently as I murmured something. I heard two people arguing, but I was too tired to catch what it was about.

"What did you do to her Nathaniel?" I heard Ash call out.

"Just help me get her to her dorm," Nathaniel said hastily.

"Not before you tell me what's going on and if she's alright," Ash said, even more pissed off.

"Look man, either help me or get out of my way, she needs to rest," Nathaniel gave back. "I didn't mean to hurt..." was the last thing I could hear before blacking out again.

"Astoria, are you alright?" I heard Hera say, bringing me back to the present.

"Yeah, I just felt a little light-headed, but I'm fine now."

"Thank god, I was worried about you! Remember you can always talk to me," she said with a genuine look in her eyes.

"Yes, thank you, now let's go on in," I said.

In reality, I was scared to go in there, knowing that I would have to face Nathaniel. *How do you even act after all of that?* People were already looking at me when I entered the room. *What did I expect? It'll get better eventually.*

It was a big room and there was a buffet spread across the whole room, it smelled delicious. We both took a plate, but I decided that I just wanted an apple and some orange juice. Truth is, I didn't feel like eating because I was still in shock about what happened yesterday.

As we were about to sit down, I heard someone yell "Astoria, Hera, come sit with us!" It was Ash, and Hera was already making her way over to them. I took a seat next to Ash and saw that the seat across from me was empty.

"Hello everyone," I said, greeting them in a tired voice.

"Are you feeling better? You looked terrible last night," Ash said in an undertone.

"Yeah, I feel better, thank you for bringing me to my dorm," I said with a slight smile, though it didn't reach my eyes.

"Nathaniel found you, you'd have to thank him – he insisted on bringing you back to your room," he told me, and I just couldn't believe this boy. *Nathaniel is such a goddamn liar.*

"Ah, here he comes, the man of the hour," Ash exclaimed, as the one person I didn't want to see walked up to us.

"Good morning everyone, Astoria," he greeted me, as if nothing happened.

He looked more handsome as ever with his suit on, and his hair was fluffier than yesterday. *How can someone so cruel look this good? It's a crime.*

"What were you whispering about?" Nathaniel asked with a grin.

"I was just telling Astoria how you saved her last night," Ash said proudly, obviously not knowing what really happened yesterday. I saw Nathaniel stiffen and clench his jaw.

"That he did, thank you for that, I appreciate it," I said with a smirk on my face, knowing that I was getting under his skin.

"What happened yesterday anyway? I didn't really understand," Ash asked suspiciously.

"Yeah, why don't you tell them Nathaniel?" I said with an even wider grin.

He put his hands on the table as if he was about to start praying. "Well, I left the party and wanted to go to my dorm, but then I saw her lying there on the floor unconscious, and even if I don't like her it would be cruel to just let her lie there, so I decided to take her to her room, where I met you Ash," he said with the most calm voice.

He was good and he knew what he was doing – he almost fooled me as well with that story. Hera saw that I was getting uncomfortable with the situation, so she changed the subject.

"Tell us Astoria, do you know any of our teachers yet?" she asked me, and honestly I hadn't had any time to even think about school, which was about to start.

"No, I have absolutely no clue," I replied.

"We'll give you a crash course. Where do we start... Do you see the man over there talking to Mr. Fray? That's Professor Mitch," Ash said while pointing to a young man in a white shirt, the type of professor you'd have a crush on, "he teaches—"

I interrupted him. "He obviously teaches history."

"You got it, now the women over here," he said, pointing towards a middle-aged woman who looked like a librarian. "That's Professor Campell, she teaches the use of light," Hera continued.

"See this bulky man over there, that's Professor McGrew, he served in the war against Aaron and his allies, and teaches defence against darkness," Hera said, pointing to a man who looked powerful and wise; he was probably around 45, but still in a great shape.

"And, of course, study of ancient runes with Mrs. Fray," Nathaniel added.

"Wait, that's it? There are only four subjects?" I asked them.

"Yes, they take it seriously and only teach the stuff that you need when it comes to magic, everything you learn here is important and could save your life," Ash explained.

I couldn't help but look over to Nathaniel now and then, only to catch him staring at me already.

I can't believe that he lies like it's nothing serious, I thought while clutching at my wrist, which still hurt.

"What's your first class, Astoria?" Hera asked me as class was about to start.

"Um wait let me see... My first class is history of magic with Professor Mitch," I said, looking at my timetable.

"Wait, Nathaniel, you have that too am I right? Why don't you accompany her?" Ash said, nudging Nathaniel. He gave me a poisonous look.

"Of course I can," he said with gritted teeth.

"We'll see you at lunch, have fun!" Ash and Hera said before leaving the dining hall.

"Now there's only us left," he said, and I couldn't quite place his tone. I packed my things and left without saying a word, but there was one problem: I didn't know where I was supposed to go.

"Astoria wait, don't be like that, I'll show you where the classroom is," he said.

"No, I don't want to be near you, you fucking liar!" I said angrily. "What's your problem with me? What could I have possibly done to make you hate me so much?"

He chuckled. "Oh god, please, you couldn't keep your pretty mouth shut and decided to tell everyone that I was at the ball," he said, now getting angry as well.

"Why wouldn't I? Are you that ashamed? I just really can't understand you, what's your deal?" I said, raising my voice.

"What's my deal? Funny, what's your deal?" he gave back sarcastically.

"You are unbelievable! I will not come with you, and don't you dare talk to me again," I threatened him.

"Stop being a brat and follow me, we'll be late for class," he said impatiently.

"Stop telling me what to do! I'm tired of getting told what to do!" I said even louder as our argument got more heated.

"Come with me now or we'll both be late!" he said. When I didn't obey, he took a step towards me and grabbed me by my wrist. I hissed at his grip on my bruised skin. He looked down at my wrist and for the first time I saw that he was shocked that he had hurt me. "I didn't mean to I swear–"

I interrupted him. "I don't want to hear any of your dumb apologies. Let's go to class," I said hastily.

He looked troubled, as if he didn't know that he hurt me. *Was it his intention to hurt me, or not?*

History

I entered the classroom and was surprised that there were so many people in one room. It seemed as if a bomb went off, and everyone was throwing things at each other.

I searched for a place which wasn't already taken, and of course the only one left was the seat next to Nathaniel. *This can't be happening, I really need to focus on my classes because I'm a beginner, and I definitely can't do that next to him.* The crowd started to sit down and calm down as the professor came through the doors.

"Hello everyone, excuse me for being late, I just had a chat with the headmistress," he said, obviously in a hurry.

As I raised my hand, Nathaniel shifted over to me and whispered, "Already tired of me I see," he said with an amused voice.

"Can you blame me?" I said with an attitude I didn't knew I had.

"Well, I certainly like a challenge, don't you?" he said.

"Oh you're on, but I swear if you even think of distracting me I'll chop your head off," I said, and almost couldn't hide my smile.

"The feeling's mutual," he said, leaning over. I shoved him back but nothing happened.

This boy is strong it's unfair. I looked over to him and there was that feeling again that I was sure was just a mistake.

The butterflies in my stomach would say otherwise. Turns out Nathaniel is an excellent student and knows much about the history of lighters.

"Alright class, split into pairs and talk about your opinion on demons," Professor Mitch said. *I knew that something like this might happen.* Nathaniel came closer to me, and I tried to put as much space between us as possible.

"What is your opinion on demons, Astoria?" he said seriously and the butterflies flipped in my stomach as I heard him say my name.

"They are bad… I guess?" I hesitated before I asked him, "What do you think about demons, Nathaniel?"

"Well, Astoria," he pointed out, "many people have died because of them, and they are a big danger especially for the first world – the history behind that isn't the thing that counts, it's how it is, and instead of learning about the history we should rather get to know more about them and how to properly kill a demon," he said surprisingly with a serious tone.

"Wow, I did not expect you to be that serious on a topic like this," I said, smirking.

He didn't say anything more and I knew that I probably shouldn't have joked about it.

Should I apologise for saying that? No, I don't owe him anything. We sat there in silence as the lesson passed by, turns out we really don't learn that much in this class.

"Now class, you are dismissed. I wish you a nice day!" Professor Mitch exclaimed, and everyone left the room in a rush. Nathaniel was already gone by the time I finished packing up, and I ran after him.

"Nathaniel!" I said loudly, hoping that he'd hear me. I'm sure he did, but he decided to ignore me. "Nathaniel, stop!" I said even louder as I grabbed him by his arm.

"What do you want Astoria?" he asked, annoyed.

"I wanted to say I'm sorry for earlier. I shouldn't have mocked you about it, but I didn't know that it was such a sensitive topic," I said, and his expression softened.

"You couldn't have known. Just please leave me alone, I don't want to be with you, do you understand?" he demanded.

"God, you really think you are better than everyone else don't you?" I said, frustrated that he distanced himself from me again.

"Get over it Astoria, you're nothing special and you don't mean anything to me, so move on. Go get your pretty boy Eden, he's head over heels for you anyways," he said in a tone I couldn't quite place. The argument was getting under my skin, so I just left him standing there.

Who does he think he is, to be so charming yet such a pain in the ass? One minute he's flirting with me and the next he's saying I don't mean anything to him. He certainly means something to me; he's hiding a secret, and I will find out what it is.

The Fight

My next class was defence against darkness. Luckily, Hera was already on her way to pick me up. "Hey girl, how was history?" she asked as she greeted me.

"It was fine. I'm just intrigued, do you know anything about Nathaniel?" I asked her as we walked towards the changing rooms.

"Well, I don't know that much, but I think his Dad died during the battle against Aaron," she said, clearly questioning my intentions.

"So you think it's possible that my parents knew his?" I said hopefully.

"It is possible, but there were many people in the battle. I'll check it out, alright?" she said sympathetically.

"Thank you, Hera, you're a good friend," I said as we arrived.

"Let's go change, and then we'll have to go to the pond," she said joyfully. I quickly changed into some black leggings, a black sports bra, and some white sneakers. As I put my hair into a ponytail I saw that Hera was already waiting for me.

"Are you coming?" she said and started running. I had no idea where I was supposed to go, so I ran after her as fast as I could.

It turned out she was even faster than I thought – by the time we reached the pond I was half out of breath and had to fix my ponytail.

"Well, ladies, I appreciate the motivation today," I heard Professor McGrew say as I looked at the beautiful view. The pond was located at the back of the academy and there was a bridge that lead across it. The pond was square, and the water wasn't the cleanest – it looked disgusting actually.

"In my class you'll learn that you have you defend yourself not only with your magic, but with your bare hands as well. I expect only the best from all of you!" McGrew told us, and I knew this class was going to be hard.

I saw two guys on the bridge start to fight, and when I took a closer look, I could tell who it was. Nathaniel's hair shimmered in the sun, and he looked like a literal angel. Ash was struggling against Nathaniel's grip, which I knew was strong. My eyes couldn't follow the fight, they were that fast! It was impressive. Nathaniel won and Ash laid on his back frowning.

"You got me this time man!" Ash exclaimed as Nathaniel helped him up.

"And that, folks, is how we do it here, good work Nathaniel," Mr. McGrew said as he patted Nathaniel's shoulder. Nathaniel looked very proud and thanked him.

"Before you ask, Professor McGrew is like a father to Nathaniel. He was in the battle where his father died and looked after him ever since," Hera whispered.

It did make sense, that's why he was that good. "Astoria! Did you see how I totally lost against this warrior here?" Ash exclaimed as he saw me.

"Yeah, it was impressive, I have a lot to learn," I said as I realised how true that was.

"Nathaniel could help you," Ash said as he looked over to him.

"We'll get partners assigned. Maybe next time," Nathaniel said disinterestedly.

I hope I'll get partnered with Hera or Ash, they are both nice and they'll go easy on me.

"Okay folks, I'll assign each of you a partner that you'll have to train with. This person will be your partner in the final exam as well," Mr. McGrew said, and I prayed for a good partner.

"Alright kids: Hera, you'll partner up with Ash, and Nathaniel will teach you everything, Astoria; he's our best, you're in good hands," he said as he looked over to the boy he raised. *Why am I not surprised? This is going to hurt a lot, thanks.*

"Just so you know, I'm not amused with the decision either, but I want a good grade on this exam so watch and learn," he said, getting up onto the bridge.

"No, Nathaniel, can't we start on the ground?" I said with a sigh.

"I won't go easy on you just because you're new. You won't succeed unless you push yourself to your limits," he said, offering me a hand.

I grabbed his hand and pulled as hard as I could, and he fell down off the bridge. "Don't underestimate me, pretty boy," I said, giving him a hand.

"I must say, I did not expect that. You might have potential after all," he said, getting up on the bridge.

"Let's test your theory," I said, getting onto the platform as well.

"You ready?" he asked, getting into the fighting stance.

"As ready as you are," I said, mirroring his movements.

He didn't strike, so I took the opportunity and punched him in his face which hurt more than I thought. Faster than I realised he put my arm behind my back and kicked into my leg so I fell over.

"Ouch," I frowned, staying on the ground.

"You're all talk," he smirked as he helped me up.

I used the chance and threw him over my back, putting my shoe on his neck while he was on the ground.

"Think again," I said, smirking.

"You definitely know how to push my buttons. You're on, but don't go crying to your friends when I destroy you," he said, definitely not joking. *Oh, I think I've made a huge mistake.* I didn't want to be seen as weak, especially not in front of Nathaniel, so I put on my poker face and went into position.

"Give me all you've got." I regretted that the second it flew out of my mouth. He came at me and punched me in the ribs and the cheek. Suddenly he was behind my back, his muscular core pressed into my back. I tried to budge but I had no chance, he was too strong.

"You can't handle me, princess," he said as he threw me over his back and I landed on the hard and cold surface.

My vision was blurry as I tried to stand up.

"Nathaniel, you arsehole, can't you go easy on her for once?" I heard Hera scream. She came and helped me up. I leaned on her for support as we walked past him.

"I can see why you couldn't help her," he exclaimed in arrogance.

"What did you just say to me?" I screamed as I rushed in his direction, getting angrier with every step.

"No wonder she died if you can't even defend yourself," he said again.

"You are unbelievable!" I said, shoving him towards the edge of the bridge.

"I bet she—" That was enough.

I pushed into his chest with all the strength I had left, and he fell into the pond with a satisfying splash. I made my way up to Hera and she excused us both from class.

Fine Line

"Astoria, what's your deal with Nathaniel?" Hera asked as we walked to the changing rooms.

"If only I knew, he hates me but then he doesn't? I can't seem to understand why he is so obsessed with me," I said thoughtfully.

"I don't think he hates you, Astoria, he would avoid you if he hated you," she said.

"Well, it wasn't his idea to be partnered up with me, just like it wasn't to walk me to class and everything else. So yes, I do think he hates me," I said as I sat down on a bench.

"Ash told me you saw Nathaniel at your ball back in Ilimara?" she asked me as she checked my leg.

"Yes, I bumped into him and he said that he'd see me soon. He even knew my name, even though I've never seen him in my entire life", I explained.

"Nathaniel hates royals, especially the ones in Ilimara, that's why nobody believed you when you told us. It's not like him."

That makes a lot of sense. But why did he spend time with me if he hates us that much? What did we do to make him hate us? "It's time to find the truth. Tell me Hera, where do they keep things they'd like to keep a secret from us?" I asked as I changed into my regular clothes.

"Come on, I'll show you," she said, and she led me through several buildings.

"This is an abandoned building where they store everything from the beginning of the founding of the academy, I'm sure you'll find something there," she said, pointing in the direction of a dark and mysterious building I'd never seen on my way around.

"I'll make sure nobody sees us, you go ahead and see what you can find," she said.

Alright it's time to find the well needed truth. I decided to try picking the lock, I had a lot of practice from sneaking out. To my surprise, it actually worked, and I opened the heavy doors. There were several cabinets and a staircase that lead down to a locked door. I decided to start where I was and make my way through everything.

It was dusty and smelled unpleasant. The only light the room got was from a tiny little window. I saw pictures of older graduates from the academy and some photos of the teachers together, as well as many books and pieces of paper. It seemed as if nobody had been in here for a very long time. I browsed through many pages of the books and saw pictures of demons until I stumbled upon a page on which I saw something different.

It looked barbaric, a creature, a fine line between human and demon. I couldn't take my eyes off of it. I tore it out of the book and put it into my pocket.

I heard Hera whistle and knew it was time to go. I grabbed a book to take with me. It looked old and hoped it would help me find my answers.

"It's time to go Astoria, did you get what you were looking for?" Hera asked as we walked towards our building.

"Not really but I got something that looked special, here, look," I said as I gave her the picture I took with me.

"What on earth is that creature? That looks horrible!" she said as she gave me the picture back.

"I don't know, but I will find out," I said as we arrived at our dorm. "Do you think anyone knows anything about them?" I asked Hera, knowing that she knew a lot of people.

"Hmm, well I guess Nathaniel would know, but knowing the history of you two I wouldn't suggest going to him. You could try it with Ash, maybe he'll convince Nathaniel to help you." That more than answered my question.

"Why does everything in my life lead me back to him? I hate that guy and he doesn't like me either, it sucks!" I complained.

"You don't have to go to him. Maybe it's nothing and the drawing was just some sketching from an artist," she said.

"You're right, I don't and I won't, nothing will lead me back to him," I exclaimed with a long sigh. "I need to get my mind off things. I'll go on a run in the forest if you don't mind?" I asked her, putting my running clothes on.

"Go ahead but please stay safe, you never know what you'll stumble across out there," she said, busy reading a book.

I left the room and made my way to the forest. I saw Nathaniel and I'm pretty sure he saw me as well, but I just walked straight past him into the forest.

It was still bright outside and the leaves had started to change their colour to red. It was a dream. I started to run, and I felt more powerful than ever. I ran until I noticed that it was beginning to get darker by the second. I decided to go back to the academy and started running again.

I heard a voice whisper in the wind, "Astoria, please find me."

I couldn't just leave – I thought it was the voice of my mother. I turned around in confusion, *it can't be right? How would that be possible?* Then I heard it again, and again. *What if it's her? Would she be disappointed in me?* I followed the voice, and I was sure that it had to be my mother. It led me through the forest, and I felt a presence getting closer.

There she was, my beloved mother, looking at me like I was a failure.

"Astoria, I don't blame you for the things that happened that night," she said, but I thought her voice was a little off. I wasn't sure what I should tell my mom. Nothing could make it better or change the way things went down that night.

"I don't just blame you for that night, I blame you for everything that happened to me. It's all your fault," she said calmly as my eyes began to water.

"No, stop Mom, I'm sorry for what happened, I miss you everyday," I exclaimed as she came closer.

"It's too late for that, look what they did to me!" she screamed, and suddenly it was dark. I heard a screech and a growl. Out of nowhere it was bright again and I was blinded for a second until my eyes adjusted to the light.

Then I saw her...the once beautiful queen, now an ugly creature. I remembered seeing this creature in the drawing I took with me. *My own mother wouldn't attack me, would she?* Then I remembered that this creature probably wasn't my mother anymore, just an empty creature without any feelings. Suddenly it sprung at me with immeasurable speed.

Deep Wounds

I was torn, she was my mother after all. I just stared at it, running towards me, I couldn't do anything. I was in shock, *my own mother is attacking me and I can't hurt her, not again.*

It sprung at me and it was on top of me, growling and screaming at me. A hot pain ripped through my chest as it scratched me with its long claws. I felt as if I couldn't breathe. Suddenly the creature backed down and screamed.

I coughed hard as the pressure suddenly left my body. I felt someone next to me, helping me sit up. "Did it hurt you?" Nathaniel asked. Before I could answer, the creature ran toward us again and he threw a ball of magic towards it, but it didn't seem to reach it.

I quickly stood up pushing away the thought that I'm bleeding heavily from my chest. "Astoria it is time for you to find out what kind of lighter you are!" Nathaniel screamed as he tried to distract the creature. I tried to build my magic up, thinking about things that make me furious.

I thought about Aaron and how he killed my mother, Eden, who just left me at an unknown place, Nathaniel, who treated me like an idiot, and everyone lying to my face the whole time.

The rage in me got stronger and I felt a tingling feeling flow through my veins. I saw that my hands were covered in some kind of dust that looked like the night sky. I knew I had to concentrate on converting it into a ball in order for it to be easier to throw.

I tried concentrating, my surroundings got brighter and my eyes were almost blinded by the bright light that came from my palms. "Astoria, please hurry up, I can't distract it any longer!" Nathaniel screamed over the creatures screams.

I tried, but I just couldn't get myself to throw my magic at it. *What if it's my mother and we can save her?*

"No Nathaniel, I'm sorry but I can't," I said, frustrated.

"For the love of god, why can't you just do something right for once in your life?" he screamed at me. "Give me your hand," he said, but I didn't react. "Astoria, give me your hand if you want to stay alive," he said, grabbing my hand.

He murmured something and a giant ball appeared in front of us, one side black, the other like the colour I saw before on my hands. It got bigger, growing until it was the size of us both.

"Nathaniel, what are you doing?"

"Just trust me," he said.

"How can I trust you after everything you've done until now?" I asked him as a little chuckle flew out of my mouth. Hilarious of him to say that I should trust him, of all people.

"Guess you'll just have to," he said and threw the ball at the creature. It screeched and screamed as I covered my ears against high-pitched sound. The creature fell to the ground and transformed into something.

I started walking towards it slowly. "Astoria stop, you don't know what you're doing," Nathaniel said as he tried to stop me. I stood over the creature only to find out that it wasn't a creature but my mother.

"Mom... No... This can't be true," I said over and over again as I moved her hair out of her face. I started feeling nauseous and I couldn't see straight anymore. I felt as if I was floating and then I fell to the hard ground covered in moss.

I woke up and saw that I was moving, somebody was carrying me. "Nathaniel..." I whispered as my eyes darted back and forth.

"Don't move, you have a bad wound on your chest and you're about to bleed out," he said and I thought I heard a little bit of panic in his words.

"We'll have to go to Mrs. Fray, she'll know what to do," I said with all the strength I had left.

"No, we can't, Astoria you don't know what that means and what we had to deal with, they can't know," he said as we got out of the forest. It was almost midnight. I was unconscious now and then but woke up several times.

He snuck us through the back door of the building and led me to an old weapons room. It was locked but he used his magic to open it. *God I'll have to ask them how they do that, it's amazing.* It wasn't a big room, there was just a bed and some cabinets. He laid me down on the bed and lit a candle. I was cold and shivered as he touched my forehead.

"Shit, the wound must be infected already because you have a high fever." He covered me with a blanket.

"Thanks…" I stuttered. He searched in vain for some bandages. He opened every drawer and made a mess, but there was nothing to be found.

"Here, take my shirt," he said as he pulled his shirt over his head in one swift motion. Beneath it I could see his muscles, and in the candlelight he looked like a Greek god.

"This will hurt, but you need to put pressure on it and just stay conscious until I come back," he said as he pressed his shirt to my open wound. He looked at me one last time before trying to find something to stop the bleeding.

I put as much pressure on as I could, but I felt the strength leave me with every minute he didn't come back.

"Astoria, how could you let him kill me? I am your mother!" I heard a voice scream. The image of my mom appeared in front of my eyes, and I remembered it all over again: The night at the castle, the nightmares I've had, and the incident that happened tonight. It felt as if I was sucked into an endless spiral of guilt. The voices in my head were getting louder and there were more and more. The only thing I heard was my mom yelling for help and choking to death.

"Astoria!" I heard a voice yell. I woke up and sat straight up, gasping for breath. My breaths came fast and shallow. I couldn't catch my breath and it hurt as I panicked.

"Astoria, calm down, it's alright," Nathaniel said as he put my head down onto the pillow again. "Breath in…" he said as I took a deep breath that hurt, "…and out," he said, and I breathed out. "I found some things that could help, but you have to sit up, can you do that for me?" he asked.

"I'm not sure, but I'll try," I said quietly as he helped me sit up.

"Now lean back and rest your back on the bed railing," he said, guiding me to it. I hissed in pain as I adjusted to the new position.

I groaned as he took his shirt away from the wound and examined it. "Ouch," I groaned as he accidentally brushed my wound.

"I'll disinfect the wound so you won't get an infection. This is going to hurt, so take this and bite on it so you don't bite off your tongue," he said, passing me his leather bracelet as he prepared the bandages.

I put it in my mouth, biting hard on it. "Three, two..." and with that he splashed the liquid over my chest. I screamed into the bracelet as I twitched in pain.

My lungs feel like they are on fire and every breath I take hurts more.

"You're doing great, I'll have to take off your shirt to put the bandages on, so this could hurt," he said as he got closer to me. His face brushed against me, his hair tickling my face as he bared my chest. He smelled amazing yet mysterious. I took his scent in and closed my eyes.

He wrapped the bandage around my body and traced a line with his finger that made me shiver. He looked handsome in this light and the way he seemed to care about me and looked after me tonight surprised me. Suddenly I wasn't cold anymore.

He sat down next to me, and I didn't know what to do. I didn't feel any pain anymore, just the desire that had been hiding inside me since the first time I laid my eyes on him.

Suddenly a wave of pain hit me and I collapsed into myself. He stabilised my body with his hand around my waist and one on the side of my neck. We looked each other in the eyes and the tension grew with every second that passed.

"Astoria...", he whispered softly before crushing his lips against mine. He was burning with passion, as was I. I put my hands on his shoulders as I turned over and sat on his lap. I kissed him harder each time our lips met, until he hovered over me and took control.

"Ouch," I shrieked as the sharp pain in my chest returned. I felt my vision go blurry as I fell unconscious once again.

Home

"Is she awake?" I heard someone say.

"Can you hear me, Astoria?" I heard another voice say. My eyes fluttered open, and I felt my head ache.

"You are awake!" I heard a voice say, recognising that it was Hera.

"You scared us, Astoria!" I recognised Ash's voice as I tried to get up.

"Don't let her move, she needs to rest before we get the Xenji from Mr. Fray's office," I heard Nathaniel say as he came closer.

I remembered everything from last night clearly, and I couldn't believe that it actually happened. He leaned closer to me to examine my wound, and his hair fell in front of his face. It looked as soft as a cloud.

How can he look that good after last night? I was pretty sure I looked flustered, and the face that Hera was making confirmed my suspicion.

"Hera, can you get the Xenji as soon as possible, I don't know if she will survive much longer," he said as he inspected every inch of my chest closely.

"Umm, about that – I don't think I can get it alone, you guys have to come with me," she said, embarrassed.

I grabbed Nathaniel's hand as he was about to leave. "Please stay with me, I don't want to be alone," I said quietly as I held onto his wrist. He brushed my hand off and left without saying anything.

My eyes were hurting so I closed them and drifted off to sleep. I don't know how much time had passed but it was getting dark again when I woke up and tried to look out the window from my bed. I went to put the curtains out of my way when I realised that my veins were turning black and it was spreading to my whole arm. *What is happening?* I panicked.

I was panting and out of breath as I laid there, not being able to do anything to stop it. *No stop it, please,* I repeated in my head as I felt it spreading. *I can't breathe.* I felt as if I was being choked. My body trembled as I gasped for air over and over to no avail. I felt the room spinning as black spots started to consume my eyesight.

"They're too late," I whispered into the wind as I took a last breath.

I woke up in the bed again, but when I tried to brush my hair out of my face my hand just went through it. *What is happening to me?* I thought sadly, though I already assumed what had happened.

"Astoria, you're finally home," a high voice said.

I turned around and saw a man standing next to me, with wings as big as I was. I felt as light as a feather.

"Are you an angel?" I asked without feeling anything, just the secure feeling of his presence.

"Why yes, I am. Angel Azrael, the angel of the death."

"Oh…" I said sadly, the truth weighing heavy upon me.

"Don't fear Astoria, I will try to delay your departure as long as possible, you deserve to see your friends one last time," he said with a sympathetic look on his perfect face. I admired his beauty and the presence that he radiated. *He doesn't look like the angel of death.*

The door suddenly opened, and there they were. I didn't hear anything; I only saw their screams and tears as they shook my dead body. It was miserable to see my friends that heartbroken and comforting each other.

They will feel responsible for my death their whole lives and they will suffer because of me. It was not their fault, they did everything they could. They were there for a long time until Nathaniel left the room quickly.

"Follow him, Astoria, but I can't guarantee you that you will make it back in time," Angel Azrael said as he sat next to my body. I wanted to open the door, but I remembered that I couldn't do that anymore. I walked through the door and into Nathaniel's room.

It was clean and everything was in its place. I heard a soft sob as I entered to room and saw him standing there, his face in his hands. "No!" he screamed as he grabbed the chair and threw it. He made a mess and was destroying everything in his room. I didn't think it would hurt him that much; after all, he did reject me again.

"Fuck," he said loudly as he saw the mess he made in his hurt and anger. All the books were on the floor, the shelf was broken, and his things were everywhere. "Why did you leave me? I need you!" he sobbed. I took his leather bracelet from my wrist and looked at it, the memory of my last night on earth.

I wished I could comfort him and tell him that everything would be alright, but I couldn't. He stood up and walked over to the window and looked out. The sun was setting, the whole sky was golden, and the light reflected on his caramel skin.

"How could you leave me? I wanted to tease you, show you how much I like you, but now you'll remember me as the demon who took your heart, only to shatter it," he murmured into the evening sun.

He sat down and picked up a piece of paper and started writing something.

"I'll remember you in every shooting star I see, every birthday candle I'll blow out, and every sunset that I'll admire," he wrote.

I put my hand on his cheek and wiped the tear away. He turned my way and looked me in the eyes. *Is it possible that he can see me or feel my presence? Why was I able to touch him?*

Angel Azrael appeared next to me and my questions were forgotten. "Are you ready to go home?" he asked me, putting a hand on my shoulder. Nathaniel left in a hurry and ran out the the door screaming something.

"Astoria? It is time to go, she's expecting you," he said again, as I stared at what Nathaniel had written. "Give me your hand, I'll guide you home."

"I'm ready to go home," I said. With one last look at my wrist, I gave him my hand.

Comfort

"Welcome home, Astoria."

"Mom!" I exclaimed as I saw her standing on the porch in front of a beautiful mansion.

"I was waiting for you," she said as she wrapped me into a tight hug.

"Mom, he killed you in the woods, didn't he?" I asked her painfully.

"Yes, I had convinced Azrael to send me back just once, so yes, he did," she answered. "I missed–"

"Astoria!" Someone shook me back and forth. I gasped for air as I finally was able to breathe without any pain. I opened my eyes and saw all of my friends staring at me in disbelief – including Nathaniel.

"You killed her!" I screamed in anger. I sprung at him, but Ash was faster.

"Astoria, stop! For the love of god, you were dead, and the first thing you do is scream at Nathaniel?"

"He killed my mother, I was there, she told me!" I growled.

"What?!" Hera exclaimed.

"It was a burned one, that creature wasn't your mother!" Nathaniel defended himself.

"She told me that you did!" I said, still struggling against Ash's hold.

"There was a burned one in the forest?" Ash asked as he let me loose.

"Not a normal one. It was transforming into a person she fears," Nathaniel said as he gave Ash a significant look.

"They're back?" Ash exclaimed in disbelief.

"Stop saying things we don't understand! What are burned ones?" Hera asked.

"They are in-between mundane and demon, humans that were possessed by demons. When they fought them, the demons burned them to get a better hold on them. There are many of them, but the one you two saw in the woods was a very rare one," Ash explained.

"They are called ferals, and they can change their appearance into the one you fear most," Nathaniel continued. "I'm guessing that Aaron sent them after you, that's why you heard them calling to you."

"Why would I fear my mother?" I asked them.

"Well, you were probably still traumatised from what happened to her," Nathaniel answered. *And because I failed her,* I thought bitterly.

"Can you guys give us a minute please?" Hera asked the boys.

"Of course. I'm really glad to have you back, Astoria," Ash said before they both left the room.

"It's time for you to tell me the truth. What happened last night?" she demanded.

"Well, you know the beginning; I couldn't bring myself to attack my mother, but Nathaniel came and helped me. He brought me back and took care of me. He cleaned my wound in the weapons room, and then I passed out and had this nightmare. He helped me calm down, and then I woke up here."

I didn't tell her about the kiss because I didn't know how to feel about it. *I'm not sure what to think of it, and I'm pretty sure he isn't either.*

"Whatever it is between the two of you, he seemed lost when we found you dead. He was a mess," she said, sitting down next to me.

"I saw it, I saw it all," I whispered as the tears came flooding up at the memory of their faces.

"I'm so sorry," Hera exclaimed before taking me into her arms and hugging me. "I think you need to have a talk with Nathaniel, he's overwhelmed by the whole situation," she said as she stood up.

I got up and took a much-needed shower, the sweat from the last two days resting on my skin, then got dressed. I decided to wear an almost nude-coloured skirt that hugged my curves softly and a sage green knitted sweater, which I tucked into my bra so it was hanging to my waist. I put my star necklace and some pearl earrings on as I left the dorm room.

"Good luck!" Hera called after me. I knocked on Ash and Nathaniel's dorm door and Ash answered.

"Is Nathaniel here?" I asked him right away.

"No, I think he went to the pond in the back to cool down. I'm busy cleaning our room after the breakdown he had."

"Thank you, for everything," I said as I left to make my way to the pond. I searched the yard until I saw him sitting on top of a hill, deep in thought.

I wasn't sure if I should disturb him, but then, I did need some answers.

I sat next to him quietly as I saw what he was looking at. There were several fireflies flying around, playing with each other. We sat there in a comfortable silence as we watched them have fun.

"You know…I was really scared when I thought I lost you," he said, breaking the silence. His eyes were glistening as he tried to look away.

"I know, I was there," I said, laying a comforting hand on his arm.

"I felt you, that's why I went back and tried again," he answered.

"Did you mean it? What you wrote in the letter?" I asked him cautiously, not knowing how he would react.

"Yeah, I did," he answered. I put my head on his shoulder and we sat there in silence, listening to the wind howling.

Back to Normal

The sunlight shone through the blinds, soon consuming the whole room. "Wake up sleepyhead, time to go to school!" Hera said happily.

"Ugh, no, don't you know I died yesterday?" I answered her, rolling over to face the wall.

"Oh please, as if I could forget! But life goes on," Hera said, pulling the blanket off me.

"It's cold, stop that!" I said as I felt the cold breeze on my skin.

"We're meeting the boys downstairs, hurry up," she said.

How could I forget? After the things we've been through, of course we're all friends now. It's great, but the tension between Nathaniel and me is still there and it weighs on all of us.

"Alright, I get it, I'll get changed and I'll meet you downstairs in a minute," I said while taking my clothes off the rack. I chose to go for an all-white outfit today – a matching cardigan and skirt set, with a white shirt.

I put my hair into a half up-do and was ready to go. I walked through the corridors as fast as I could without looking stupid and arrived at the dining hall.

It smelled delicious as I took a tray and made my way to the buffet. Pancakes, all kinds of fruits, and eggs, you could have it all. I took some pancakes and a couple of strawberries and went to our usual table.

"Good morning everyone!," I said cheerfully.

"Why are we so happy today?" Ash asked, smiling.

"Well, about the little things that I would've missed if I died yesterday!" I explained.

"Yeah, we certainly are glad that you are here, you scared the hell out of us though," Hera said before taking a sip of her orange juice. "What's on your agenda today?"

"I think the use of light and ancient runes," I said, not sure because I didn't memorise my schedule.

"Ah, great, so you're with me today," Ash said happily before finishing his apple, "and with Nathaniel."

"Alright then, what are we waiting for?" I asked them, saying goodbye to Hera. *I'll give Nathaniel his space and just let him be, I don't want our friend group destroyed again.* "Where is the classroom?"

"It's the building next to our dorms, so it's not that far," Nathaniel answered as we stepped outside.

I missed a step and almost fell down the stairs. My books and notes all fell to the ground, and I bent down to pick them up.

Nathaniel came to my help and gave me a little smile. "You're welcome," he said as he gave me my things back.

"Come on you two, I want to get the good seats and not the bad ones," Ash said as he started to walk faster, leaving us behind.

"There are bad seats?" I asked as a light chuckle escaped my mouth.

"Yes, Astoria, there are, the ones in the middle are for losers," Ash explained to me as we tried to catch up.

"That's hilarious. So you're either a nerd and sit in the front, or you're an even bigger loser if you sit in the back?"

"We normally sit in the front because we don't like the people in the back," Nathaniel said with a scowl.

Seems like he just doesn't like people at all. "What's up with them?" I asked them both, intrigued.

"They're the worst, they bully people and lie to them – all the gossip comes from them," Ash answered, not looking very pleased.

"You have to keep an eye out for James. I know he can be charming, but he is dangerous," he continued as we walked into the classroom.

"Astoria! How have you been, I heard you didn't feel well?" Mrs. Fray asked me as she saw me.

"Yeah, I guess I was overwhelmed with the whole situation," I lied.

"Well, I'm glad that you're feeling better because my class will be an important one for sure," she said, smiling. "I reserved you some seats, I know how you two hate sitting in the back," she said to the two boys graciously.

"Thank you, ma'am!" Ash exclaimed happily as he sat down.

"Astoria, my dear, is there something you want to tell me?" she asked me with a questioning look.

"Oh, no, everything's alright, I'll let you know if something happens, I promise," I assured her, knowing that I'd do no such thing. *I'm not sure why they don't trust her, I'll have to investigate.*

I heard the door open and saw a beautiful boy walk in. He had dark hair and was well dressed. He gave me a smirk and sat down in the back of the classroom.

"Hey, who's that boy in the back?" I asked them, pointing in his direction.

"James, the one we warned you about earlier. Don't you dare talk to him." Nathaniel scowled and turned back around.

"Why would I not talk to him? He's in my class."

Nathaniel stiffened. "Do not do it, Astoria. It's for your own good, trust me," he ordered.

"Welcome, my dears! Today we'll learn about the rune used for unlocking," Mrs. Fray told us, and I turned my attention back to her. "Can someone explain to Astoria what runes are for?" she asked the class. A few people raised their hands. "James, enlighten her," she said.

"Hello, Astoria," he said with a wink, "Runes can help us cast a spell, but only if you know how to use them. Once your magic is activated, you can draw a rune with your hand, which makes spellcasting faster and more effective," he explained.

"And it's safer," Mrs. Fray added. "Runes are crucial in the journey of learning how to use our magic. There are more runes than you can count, but we will learn their benefits and how to use them. Welcome to the class," she said, and the lesson started.

"For example, there is the healing rune," she drew a triangle on the board, "which can speed up the process of healing certain wounds." She cut herself with a piece of paper and drew the rune with her hand. The papercut suddenly disappeared. *That is amazing! And it's useful; I guess that's what they did to me when I was dying.*

"Another example is the binding rune: it connects two people when they are very serious with each other, kind of like giving an everlasting promise," she explained, showing us the rune on her skin.

"There are certain runes which we carry on our skin, but most of the time we just draw them in the atmosphere and they disappear," she explained.

For the rest of the class, I listened closely and learned so many new things that I felt like I had to go and take a nap right away.

"Hey boys, can I head back and go take a nap?" I asked them as we were packing up our stuff.

"No Astoria, we have classes in 15 minutes. Come on, you'll survive if we have all this time," Ash answered, and we went out of the building.

"Hey Nathaniel, how have you been brother?" I heard James yell as he came up to us. *Uh oh.* I sensed that this wouldn't end well as I saw everyone tense up.

"Astoria do you have a minute?" he asked, smirking.

"Leave her alone," Nathaniel said in a calm but cautious voice.

"Chill, I just want to talk to her," James said, "I won't hurt her like you do."

Nathaniel clenched his jaw. "Leave her be and we won't have a problem," he said, stepping in front of me.

"Stop telling her what to do, you obviously don't know what's best for her," James said jealously.

Nathaniel grabbed his shirt and punched him.

"Stop it!" I said, getting between them. "It"s fine, I want to talk to him, stop being such a prick." Nathaniel left.

"I am so sorry about that, but you shouldn't have provoked him," I apologised.

"Astoria, it's fine, he can't treat you like that you know? It's not his decision to make," he said as he cleaned the blood off his face.

"Let me help you," I said, opening my purse and taking out a tissue. "Come here." He stepped closer and I gently wiped his skin with the tissue.

"What do you say, doctor? Will I survive?" he said, clenching his teeth.

"I wouldn't count on it, you're living awfully dangerously," I smiled.

"What's life without a little fun and danger, right?" he said with a spark in his eyes. He stood up and brushed my hair out of my face, and with a smirk he said, "Find me if you want to know the truth about Aaron."

I knew there was something about him. He knows how to charm a girl. And he certainly succeeded with me.

The Art of Convincing

I quickly found the way to my next class – luckily I wasn't too late. I sat next to Ash and Nathaniel, catching my breath.

"Astoria–"

I interrupted Nathaniel. "I don't want to hear it, he is not as bad as you think he is," I said, trying to convince him.

"Just remember: we warned you, but you didn't want to listen," said Ash.

"Oh, come on Ash, really? You're taking his side?" I refused to take that talk seriously. *It's ridiculous, I can talk to whoever I want.*

"Yes, I am. You don't know what he's done, he has a bad reputation for a reason," he explained, not convincing me in the slightest.

"I guess we'll find out. At least he can give me the answers I've been seeking," I said, stubborn.

"Can he?," Nathaniel said sarcastically.

Before I could respond, the doors opened and light filled the room. Suddenly a woman was standing in front of the class.

"I'm Professor Campell, your teacher for the use of light. If you study hard enough and pay attention, you will be able to do what I just did and so much more," she said sternly.

"Astoria, how do you use your magic?" she asked, intrigued.

Why did she pick me? My heartbeat sped up and I didn't know what to respond.

"Well, how did you cast your magic in the past?" she asked again. *Great question, much better.*

"I was furious and angry and then it just happened," I answered shyly.

"Correct. Our magic is linked to our emotions and thoughts. The happier you are, the stronger your magic gets," she told the class.

"In my class we'll also learn about the different elements, the things your magic can do, and the consequences," she said. "There were six in total but now there are only five." She chose some students to come forward.

"What happened to the sixth?" I asked.

"They all died in the big battle, back in the days when the lighters and demons were at war. We've never seen one since," she answered sadly.

"Alright, I've chosen one student per element, and I want you to show your magic to the class. Eric, you can start," she said to a boy I had seen before, in the dining room. A big drop of water appeared hovering in the air above his palm.

"The water element can control all water atoms in the atmosphere, waterfalls, rivers or even the ocean. Phoenix, go ahead," Professor Campell said to a girl with red hair, which suited her, because her element was fire. Her hands looked like they were burning, and she even lit a candle in the process.

"Fleur, step forward," the professor said to a girl who looked like she had stepped out of an indie movie. She made her way over to a plant, and suddenly it started growing bigger and bigger.

"Impressive," I muttered under my breath.

"Helio, can you give us some more light?" she asked a white-haired boy who stood in the back. The room started getting brighter, and it seemed as if the sun was shining through the stone walls. *I'm sure you could blind someone with that if you wanted to.* They all left the podium and went back to their seats. *Those were four elements, what about the fifth?*

"Would you do the honours, Nathaniel, as the only one who possesses it here in the academy?" she asked, and he hesitantly stood up. He walked up to the podium and rolled up his sleeves, and black dust with little dots appeared on his hands.

"Okay, that's more than enough Nathaniel, please go to your seat," she said, overwhelmed. *What is her problem? He just stood there and didn't even get to perform his magic.*

I didn't know that he was the only one with that kind of magic here. I'll have to ask him about that. The lesson was over, and I felt like I was getting the hang of it.

Later that day we all regrouped in mine and Hera's room and talked about the news. "I can feel them, the burned ones in the forest. It's like they're calling me," I finally said.

They glanced nervously at each other. "You can feel them?" Hera asked in disbelief.

"Yes, whenever I'm near the forest it's like they're pulling me towards them," I continued.

"Last night I saw a little girl...I couldn't help her, she didn't survive the attack," Nathaniel admitted, rubbing his neck.

Hera gasped. "Oh my god, I thought they just wanted Astoria!"

"If they did, it looks like they changed their minds; they'll take everyone they can get and won't hesitate to leave the forest. It's only a matter of time until they attack the academy," Ash told us.

"We have to do something before it's too late," I exclaimed.

"Astoria is right, we can't just watch and do nothing," Hera agreed.

"No! We can't, did you forget what happened when we were attacked? There are hundreds of them out there, we're not strong enough!" Nathaniel disagreed.

"I'm on Nathaniel's side, unless one of you is blessed with the stardust magic," Ash said sarcastically, "then we can talk about it."

"Wait, is that the sixth magic that didn't occur for thousands of years?" I asked.

"Yes, they were executed because of the things they can do with their magic. They can kill someone easily and turn them to stardust, and because of that the demons killed all of them in the war," they explained after one another.

"Well, I'm light," said Hera, "so I'm definitely not stardust. Ash is a nature, Eden is a water, James is a fire and Nathaniel is a ..."

"I'm a shadow," Nathaniel said bluntly.

"What does your magic do, Nathaniel?" The question had been burning on my tongue.

"I can do a lot of things, but I can make you feel the loss of a loved one. You'll feel like the person you love most has just died in front of you."

"That's why I felt that way that night," I said, stopping before I said too much.

"The real question is, what kind of magic do you have?" Hera asked what they all wanted to know so desperately.

"I have no clue; neither of my parents are lighters and I never really got to use it," I said.

"I would say it's time to find out. You ready?" Ash asked me.

I was more ready than they could ever be. *It's time to learn some more about myself.*

Stardust

It was already night as we stepped outside and made our way to a training field I'd never seen in the whole time I was here. There were dummies and targets, and there was a stone circle which was radiating energy.

"Alright, just step into the circle and concentrate on your magic and what you want to do with it," Nathaniel said.

When I entered into the circle I felt weird tingles all over my skin, and I could feel my magic burning inside me. I stepped into the middle and saw them all looking at me. I tried to concentrate, but nothing happened. I tried again without success. I was getting more and more frustrated as I tried numerous times without getting it right.

"Don't forget, magic is linked to your emotions! Think of something that makes you happy!" Ash called.

I thought about all the good things I'd experienced there, and the people I've met. I could feel the smile on my face getting bigger and bigger. And then it happened.

My magic appeared on my hands and was hovering above them, ready to be used, like galaxies and nebulae contained in a small flame. It was dark, but also bright and violet, with little stars that shone bright. *None of the magic I've seen the others practice looked like this, what does this mean?* It flickered, not strong enough to burn bright, and then it just burned out and disappeared.

I suddenly felt exhausted and walked back to the others, frustrated. When I finally got there I saw them all staring at me like I was an alien.

"Uh, guys, you're scaring me. What's wrong?"

"Astoria, you–" Hera tried.

"What?" I was getting more worried by the second.

"You possess stardust magic, Astoria," Nathaniel said plainly.

"Wait, what?" I exclaimed. *I need to sit down.* "But how is that possible? You said all of them were killed!"

"They were. I never would've guessed that you were one – that night in the forest I thought I had just imagined it. Now I'm sure you are," Nathaniel said, taking my hand.

"It's going to be alright, I'll help you find the answers," he said, looking into my eyes.

I've missed him. I missed his grey eyes, that sparkle he has when we're together.

"No, that's not possible, there's no way in hell that's true, how could that be possible?" Ash exclaimed, as shocked as I was. It helped a lot that Nathaniel was there for me, and I felt way better.

"Maybe her magic changed because of the encounter she had with Aaron," Hera said, trying to make it make sense.

"No, you know that's not how it works, she would be...no, that's not possible," Ash said.

"Come on, Ash, we're going to the library. Maybe we'll find something," Hera said, and they walked away.

With Nathaniel's hand still in mine, I looked over the training field. "This is impressive, it's like they're preparing us for war," I said, shaking my head.

"That's because they are," he replied, "it's only a matter of time until Aaron comes back with an army full of demons and attacks us."

"And it's all my fault. Maybe I should just leave so everyone else is safe," I said, leaning on his shoulder.

"No Astoria, if you leave I will find you and go with you", he said in a serious voice. "Woah, Nathaniel was that a love confession I just heard?", I said chuckling. "Maybe", he said while chuckling too.

"You know, I'm really sorry for how I've treated you. I was afraid because of these sudden feelings I didn't know how to handle them," he said quietly. "I thought you would hate me after all the things I've done."

"Nathaniel, nothing could make me hate you–"

I got interrupted as we heard a loud screeching coming from the forest.

"Come on, we have to go," he said, taking my arm.

"No, Nathaniel, you said I have the power to kill them, this is my chance!" I said.

"Yes, you do, but only if you know how to use your magic! You're not ready yet, come with me," he said pleadingly.

"Fine," I said. *As soon as I'm ready I'll go and kick their asses,* I thought determinedly. We ran into the building, and before we parted ways he stopped me.

"Hey, I care about you, so stop putting yourself in danger. I won't be able to protect you all the time," he said, looking down at me.

"You don't have to, I can handle myself," I argued, but amended, "but thank you, I appreciate it, I really do," while hugging him goodbye.

He left, but I didn't feel like going to bed. I was overwhelmed and didn't know how to process the fact that I possess stardust magic, so I decided to go and take a walk on the campus. I always felt connected to nature, and it helped calm me down a little bit. *My life is a mess, I never get a break from it.*

"Astoria!" I heard a familiar voice yell, though I couldn't quite place it. I turned around and saw James walk towards me. "Can't sleep either?" he asked as he greeted me with a big smile.

He looked so mysterious, and I was intrigued; I wanted to know more about him. "Yeah, kinda discovered some big things about me today and I don't know how to process it," I answered him as we walked side by side.

"You can talk to me if you want. After all, I did tell you that I have some answers for you," he said, pausing to look at me.

"My magic is different, and I just wish that I knew how to use it," I complained.

"I'll teach you, come on," he said, taking off.

Standing in the stone circle once again, he lit the candles with his fire magic.

"Alright, what they teach you is wrong and only stops you from seeing your full potential," he said. "Instead of being happy, you have to be angry and furious to access all the magic you have. Watch," he continued.

At first his palm was on fire, but the flame was about to burn out. Suddenly the flame got bigger and even his dark eyes started to turn red. It was impressive what he could do with that power. He stopped and came towards me.

"Not many people know this, because they think it's too dangerous for us to know, but the key is to be angry at something," he said with a mysterious smirk.

"Alright, let me try," I said with a smile.

I walked over and started to feel my magic burn. At first it was only a shimmer like before. I started to think about all the things that made me angry, especially Aaron. Suddenly there was a big cloud of stardust hovering above my palm. It was beautiful, you could even see the stars in it. I stopped and walked back to James.

"Wow, that was beautiful, just like you," he said, grinning.

"Thank you for showing me," I blushed.

"Let's go back. Tomorrow we can go search for the answers you've been seeking," James said. He walked me back to my dorm and we stopped outside my door.

"Thank you again for showing me, and I'd love to accept your offer," I said, smiling.

His eyes were sparkling as he looked into the depths of my soul. "Then I'll see you tomorrow," he replied, but neither of us moved.

He started to lean in, his hair brushing against my cheek as he took it in his hand. The door opened, and Hera stood there. We sprung apart and he rubbed his neck sheepishly.

"I'll see you tomorrow, Astoria," he said before leaving.

"Don't look at me like that, Hera," I said, brushing past her.

"I know James, he's not a good guy," she said, sitting down on her bed.

"How would you know?" I asked, getting a little bit angry.

"Because everyone knows! He has a bad reputation for a reason, please do yourself a favour and stop hanging out with him," she said.

I knew that she has my best interests at heart, but I didn't want to hear it. "Give him a chance! He's not that bad, he helped me today," I gave back as I sat down on my bed.

"We've warned you. Don't expect us to be there for you when something happens, because believe me, something will," she said with complete certainty.

"He's the only person who can teach me what I need and that helps me get the answers that I need," I said defensively.

"And what are we doing all the time? Are we not helping you?" Hera bristled.

I went too far, I shouldn't have said that. They've done everything for me, and what am I doing?

"Hera, that's not what I—"

"Don't waste your breath Astoria, you'll just make it worse," she said, turning her back to me. I undressed and went to bed, but I couldn't sleep, knowing that I had made a huge mistake.

Consequences

I woke up with yesterday's events fresh in my mind. James, the argument with Hera, and Nathaniel. *Now that I know how to control my magic I can finally try to kill all the demons in the forest. I have to find Nathaniel and tell him everything.*

I noticed that Hera wasn't in her bed; in fact, she was nowhere to be found. I took a shower and dressed myself up. I put my favourite mom jeans on, as well as a sage cardigan which covered most of my chest. I took my stuff and made my way to the dining hall.

It smelled delicious as always, and as I took a tray I had a hard time to decide what to take. I decided to go with a fruit bowl and a glass of water and made my way up to our table. I stopped when I saw that the table was already full; somebody else had taken my place. *Was the argument that bad? I didn't mean to lash out at her, but I thought it would be okay.*

I saw Nathaniel look over to me, avoiding my eyes. He seemed disappointed.

Who do they think they are, to tell me who I can hang out with? Ash didn't look at me at all and tried to distract himself with talking to the others.

I stood there for a moment, then turned around to sit at an empty table. My fruit just tasted like water now. Sometimes one of them would look over to me, and I didn't know how to act. Suddenly, someone called my name.

"Astoria, how are you?" James asked, approaching me. He sat down beside me and I regretted my food choice the second I saw his delicious pancakes.

"Hey James! I'm fine, how are you?"

"Well, you don't seem fine. What's bothering you?" he asked, munching on his pancakes. I stayed quiet, and knew that James sitting with me would be an even bigger issue.

"Okay, I get it. I take it that whatever it is is the reason you're sitting alone?" he asked archly.

"Yes, it is, actually," I said dryly, folding my hands together and resting my head on them.

"What's your first class for today, Astoria?" he asked over the last of his pancakes.

"I have history," I yawned. It's true, history was really boring, but Nathaniel had made it survivable. I felt sick at the thought that I might've lost him and the rest of my friends because of some random boy I met.

But that boy can help me more than they could, and they have to understand that I need to take that into account. Suddenly I had an idea.

"Hey James, can you teach me more things today after school?"

A smile spread across his face. "Of course, meet me at the abandoned building after school?"

"It's a date," I said with a fake smile. Now that I'd lost my friends, I could at least try to make the best of the situation and take advantage of James' knowledge. I stood up and went into the corridor.

"Hey, Astoria!" I heard Ash call after me. *Great, someone else who's mad at me.* I stopped in my tracks and turned around. He looked exhausted. He quickly approached me and looked around to make sure no one was watching.

"Give them time to get over it, they are used to people using them and then leaving," he said genuinely.

"I'm not sure if I can make it right, you have to understand me, James knows things nobody else does. I don't like him, but I need to know more about all of that," I said, trying to make him understand.

"I know you would never betray us, Astoria, don't worry. They'll see that too someday," he said with a sad smile.

"How's Nathaniel doing?" I asked, worried.

"He's in pretty bad shape, Astoria. He hasn't eaten since yesterday, and he was up all night. He's closing up again, but I don't think anyone can get back inside this time."

"Oh." It was my fault, all of it. *He trusted me, and now he's closing up again.* "I'm so sorry, Ash. Please give me time, I'll try to make it right again," I said and went in for a hug.

"I think it's better if we don't do that," he said, avoiding my arms. "Goodbye, Astoria," he said, turning around and walking away.

I hate myself. Why do I hurt the people that care about me? I have to talk to Nathaniel. He won't understand what I'm doing, but I have to tell him that I don't like James and that nothing is happening between us.

When I stepped into the classroom some of the students were already sitting and chatting. I saw Nathaniel talking and laughing with someone. He seemed alright and happy, but hid face fell when he noticed me. He was clearly angry and disappointed, but the next moment he looked fine, as if nothing happened. I chose to sit in the back and let him be happy. *Why does he seem fine? I need to talk to him.*

I sat alone in the back, and wasn't listening to the Professor. I was too busy thinking about what I'd done and what I should do. *Is all of this worth it in exchange to know more about me and why I am what I am? I'm not so sure anymore.* The lesson was over, but I was still lost in my thoughts.

I came back to reality and heard people talking happily as they left the building. I got my stuff together and saw Nathaniel brush past me. I wasn't sure if I should talk to him. *What would I even say?* I took my stuff and followed him outside.

"Nathaniel!" I yelled over the voices of the students. He turned around, but in the same moment I heard someone yell my name. I saw James approaching us, and my stomach sank. A wave of regret spread across Nathaniel's face, and he turned around and walked in the other direction.

"I'm sorry, did I interrupt something important?" James asked concernedly.

"No, it's alright, are you ready?" I asked him, smiling.

"Let's go," he said, taking my hand.

Maybe he isn't as bad as everyone says, he's never done anything to hurt me and I'm sure he never would. Nathaniel will never be able to forgive me for what I did, and maybe that's for the best.

We walked in silence for a little while, until James took a deep breath.

"So, Astoria, what do you want to know exactly?" he asked me with a smirk.

"I want to know everything about Aaron and the burned ones," I said, driving off my thoughts. *I need to have the answers I've been seeking to destroy them and kill Aaron. He's the only one that knows what I'm searching for.*

"We'll find the answers you're looking for, I promise," he said, giving my hand a little squeeze.

Way Back

We arrived at the abandoned building I had searched with Hera. "James, I was already here and I found nothing."

"Do you trust me?" he asked as he opened the heavy door.

"Yes, I do," I said. *I have to trust him.*

We stepped into the room. The smell hadn't changed since the last time I was here. It was dark, and I couldn't see anything.

"Give me a second," he said, and in one swift moment he lit all the candles that stood in the room. "I take it you searched this room, right?" he asked.

"Yes, but I found nothing but pictures of older graduates and teachers," I said.

"Then it's time to find out what secrets they're keeping from us," he said, taking the steps down to the locked door.

"You asked for answers, here they are," he said, pointing to the door. "Come on, Astoria, you can open the door with your magic," he said taking my arm and dragging me down the stairs.

"I can try," I said, unsure. I took the lock into my palm and started to concentrate.

"Think about all the bad things that happened and how they make you feel," he whispered in my ear.

Memories arose of that night in the castle, the hatred I felt towards Aaron, the anger at myself for hurting everyone close to me, at Eden for how he just left me here, all alone, at Nathaniel because he can't decide if he wants me or not. The power became stronger with every memory and feeling I had. I heard a little click sound and the lock sprang open.

I hissed as a sharp pain swept across my palm. Dropping the lock, I saw that I was burnt, as though the metal was white-hot in my palm.

"I've never seen someone hurt themselves directly from their magic. Were you thinking about yourself?" he asked, worried.

"I thought about the hate I feel towards myself," I explained.

"You should never think of yourself while using your magic, it doesn't know the difference between you and the object you're referring to. You wanted to hurt yourself," he said, stating the obvious.

"I-I don't know why I did that," I said, shocked and knowing that that was exactly what I wanted, to hurt myself.

"Hey, shh, it's fine, you can talk to me," he said, taking me into his arms. I started to sob, not knowing how to deal with the situation. I had never wanted to hurt myself before, I would never do that. I was angry at myself, yeah, but I would never intentionally harm myself.

"We can try again sometime, but I think we should take a break, come on," he said, putting his arm around my shoulders. We left the building and sat down on a bench.

"Astoria, what's going on?" he said, and the sadness came to the surface once again.

"I hurt everyone that is close to me, my mother, my friends, everyone, and I can't help it," I said, frustrated.

"That's not true, you're trying to be fair to everyone, and you're the kindest person I know," he reassured me. "After all, you gave me a chance even with the bad reputation I have," he said, putting on a smile.

"Well, you're not as bad as everyone says," I told him. *It's true; maybe I should give him a real chance.*

"I think you're the only one who sees it that way," he sighed and brushed my hair out of my face. I laid my hand on his hand, which was brushing my cheek.

"No, you just have to give them a chance and not close up," I said quietly.

"You make it sound so easy, but it's not," he said, frustrated. His eyes told me that there was so much more behind this mysterious boy than I had expected.

Out of nowhere it began to snow, and we both covered our heads with a light chuckle.

"Come on let's go back," he said, taking my hand and covering me from the falling snow. We walked through the empty hallways as our steps echoed.

"Let me be honest, I didn't have the best time today, but you made it better with your presence," I said shyly.

"I'm relieved that you were able to tell me a little bit about yourself, and I promise you I'll open up to you some more," he replied. Soon after, we arrived at my door, and the moment of tension from last night repeated.

"I'll see you soon," I told him, and hugged him goodbye. There was a hint of disappointment on his face.

I really do like him, but it's not the same as what I have with Nathaniel. I'm not ready to let that go just because I made a mistake. Maybe I should apologise to him, but I don't think it'll change anything.

I braced myself, knowing that I had to see Hera. I really was sorry for what I did, and I would do anything to make it better. I opened the door, and the familiar scent came flooding out. It gave me comfort; the good times that we had came back with the smell. She was sitting at her desk and studying; by the faces she was making, she wasn't succeeding.

Maybe we can start over? "Hey, what are you doing in my room? What's your name?" I said as she turned to face me.

"Astoria, that's not how it works and you know it," she said with a small smile.

"Please Hera, give me a chance? I really miss my best friend," I said sadly. I sat down on my bed, which was right next to the desk she was working on.

"It's not like you lost me, Astoria," she said. A huge smile spread across my face. I was so relieved that after what I did, she still wanted to be friends with me. "I can't speak for all of us – you know, what you did concerns Nathaniel, not me," she said and by the sound of her voice she wasn't over it, but she was trying.

"I know, but I don't know what I'm feeling. I never intended to hurt him," I said regretfully.

"Why are you still hanging out with James then? I don't get it, what could he possibly offer you to leave all of us like it's nothing?"

"He can give me all the answers to the questions I have! I know that you guys tried everything to help me, but he knows everything, and I didn't want to bother you anymore with my stuff," I explained.

"Did you ever think about why he knows all of that, or why he's helping you? Do you really think it's just because you need answers?" she asked sceptically.

"Of course I did, but honestly I don't care. As soon as I have my answers I'll leave him," I lied. *I like James, I really do, he's a great guy and I won't be able to just leave him like that.*

"Then I'm glad, but please be careful, I don't want to lose my best friend." She smiled and gave me a big hug.

"I missed you," I said into her hair.

"I did too, Astoria, I did too."

Rain

The days flew by as the campus was covered in snow. I hung out with James a lot; we had a great time together and we became very close. I told Hera everything about what happened with James, and she gave me the best advice she could.

She was the only one that knew I was starting to have feelings for James. I just hoped that she wouldn't tell Nathaniel, but I did trust her. I saw Nathaniel multiple times, but we never spoke; we tried to avoid each other as much as possible. I never saw Ash, but I figured he wouldn't want to talk to me.

Soon there wasn't anything more James could give me, but I still wanted to hang out with him. I really enjoyed his presence, and he was a good listener. He helped me build a stronger bond with my own magic, and since then I had improved a lot.

The situation in the forest was getting out of hand; more and more students were being reported missing. The academy prioritised defence against darkness and use of light because of the situation. The atmosphere was tense, and nobody knew what was going to happen next.

The most important thing is that nobody can know that I possess stardust magic; We don't know what they would do to me if they knew.

Hera let out a long sigh, pulling me out of my thoughts.

"What's next for you and James? And what role does Nathaniel play in it?" she asked while putting on her makeup.

"Can you please ask me something I know?" I said, shifting in bed.

"Well, it's important to know what you're feeling and what you're going to do next, don't you think?" she chided me.

"Of course it is. I'll talk to James about it today," I said, annoyed.

"Great, now come on and get ready." She grabbed her jacket and went to the door. I was dressed already, but I put on my big scarf and put my hair into a ponytail.

"It's not like we're sitting together anyways," I rushed as we neared the dining hall.

"Yes, but maybe the boys are finally over it and you can sit with us," she said hopefully.

"I'm not sure if I even want that, Hera, I have to talk to James. I'll see you later," I said as we parted ways and took the opposite doors into the dining hall.

"Hey, you," James said, hugging me from behind.

"Good morning, stranger," I replied. "I don't really have time to eat, I'm with Professor McGrew today and I have to train with him," I said, sitting down.

"Are you really sure you don't want a bite of these delicious waffles?" he said teasingly.

"You're making it hard, but I really don't have time. I'll see you after class on the training field?" I asked, standing up.

"Like every day," he said, giving me a wink.

I had to change into my training clothes on the way to Professor McGrew. He's the only professor that knows what I am and what I possess, and he offered me some extra lessons so that I'm well prepared for what's coming. He was nowhere to be found, and I made my way up to the pond.

In one swift moment he appeared in front of me and blasted me with his magic. I blocked just fast enough for my magic to collide with his, and he took a step back, impressed.

"Good timing, Astoria, just like we practiced!" he said, coming over.

"Thank you, sir, it's only because of your training," I said.

"Alright, but let's train your combat skills now. You can't always count on your magic to work in the moment," he said, making his way onto the bridge.

I remembered Nathaniel standing in the exact spot, his hair shining in the afternoon sun, the smirk he always gave me. McGrew noticed and made his way over to me.

'Hey, Astoria, don't you worry about Nathaniel, he'll get over it eventually," he assured me. *Eventually is not good enough for me.*

We trained for over two hours, until my shirt stuck to my skin. I retied my ponytail and went over to Professor McGrew.

"You did great! If you continue to train like that, there's not much Aaron can do to you," he said proudly. "You can call me Christopher if you'd like, since we do spend much time with each other," he said with a little smile.

"How is he? Nathaniel?" I asked cautiously. We never really talked about him and I wasn't sure what Nathaniel told him.

"He's surviving…he's not doing great, honestly. He told me everything, what you did really hurt him," he said, but I knew that it wasn't personal.

"I just wish there was something I could do to make it right, I never intended to hurt him in any way," I said sadly.

A wave of sympathy crossed his face as he gave my shoulder a squeeze. "I don't think there is. You're a great girl, Astoria, don't let him destroy your future," he told me as he turned away to prepare for his class.

I didn't have any classes, so I took a shower and made my way to the library.

I was convinced that there had to be something there which could help me understand how it was possible for me to have magic at all, let alone stardust magic.

There weren't many students in the library, and I took some promising books and browsed through them. The way demons hunted and killed people who possessed stardust magic was brutal.

Nobody helped them. Even though they all knew and would've been able to defeat them, nobody did. *Why would they do that to their friends and family?* It made no sense.

The drawings were brutal and inhuman. *What if some of them were my parents? There's no way for me to know; maybe that's why I got adopted.* I put the books back and made my way to training field to meet James.

My feelings were clear. *I can't be with James. I really like him, but Nathaniel is special.* The cold was biting at my nose, and I put my hands deep into the pockets of my jacket. He was already sitting on the bench, casting some spells.

"Look who finally made it," he said as I approached him.

"I'm sorry, I got carried away in the library," I explained sitting down. A few minutes passed while I summoned up the courage to say what I needed to say.

"So…did you want to talk to me about something?" he asked, breaking the silence.

"Yes, I do," I said nervously. Thankfully we were alone, and nobody was there to hear what we were talking about.

"It can't be that bad, come on," he said, grinning.

"Well, I–" I stopped, thinking about how I should say it. "I don't want to hang out with you anymore, it isn't working out for me," I said, finally.

He shifted to the other end of the bench from me. "What are you talking about, Astoria?"

"Please understand, I really enjoyed our time, but I can't keep shutting down everyone who's important to me in order to be with you," I explained.

"You don't get to decide that, Astoria, you belong to me," he said fiercely, coming closer to me.

How dare he? "I don't belong to anyone! Just go and get over it!"

"I will never let you go, you will come with me," he growled, grabbing me by the arm.

"Where do you think we're going? You sound ridiculous, James!" I tried to push his hand away, but his grip got even stronger as he took both of my wrists and looked me directly in the eye.

"Where do you think, child?" he asked, and my stomach turned to ice.

Mouth wide agape and eyes wide, I didn't fight as he took my wrists and pulled me to my feet. "You are so stupid! Why did you think I knew so much about him? You made it so easy, it was fun," he cackled.

I would've given everything for someone to be here and help me. *I never should've met him somewhere quiet.* Every part of me hated him.

"I gave up everything for you! I betrayed the only people who ever cared about me!" I yelled as loud as possible, in the hopes someone might hear.

"Oh, child, you are so naïve. Nobody will help you because you pushed them away for me! Don't you understand, it's too late," he said, clearly enjoying himself.

Hot pain shot through my entire body as he grabbed my arm once again with his inhuman grip. He was right, there was nothing I could do; everything I knew, he had taught me. He would know my every move before I made it. It really was too late.

"Get your hands off her, she's mine!"

I turned around to see Nathaniel approaching us, furious as his eyes locked on to James' hand on my arm.

"Oh, so now you're protecting her?" James taunted.

"That's all I've done from the start! Only I can lay hands on her. She's mine, only mine," he spat, blasting him with power like I'd never seen. James was thrown back, and he stayed on the ground.

Nathaniel took me in his arms and told me to wait in the weapons room. I quickly made my way to the room we had both discovered some time ago. I was worried about him. *James is powerful, I'm not sure Nathaniel can handle him. He may be able to handle everyone else but this one is different.*

I heard the door lock click and sprung out of the bed. Nathaniel's knuckles were bleeding, and his cheek was badly wounded. He was breathing heavily, and I rushed into his arms.

"Thank god you're okay," he sighed in relief.

"Why did you do that?" I asked, sitting down on the bed.

"You're my everything, I'm not letting you go," he said in a dark but vulnerable voice.

"I am so sorry, Nathaniel, for everything, I should've listened to you," I said, and my eyes began to water.

"I know, I know," he repeatedly said, putting his arm around my shoulder, comforting me.

"He won't be a problem anymore, I took care of that," he said, murmuring into my hair.

"I don't know what would've happened if you weren't there, he was working with Aaron," I said beginning to sob.

"I assumed he was, but there was nothing I could do but look after you from a distance," he said, squeezing me a little tighter.

It began to rain, droplets falling heavily on the window. "What's your favourite thing about the rain?" I asked.

He shifted away from me a little. "What?" he asked.

"What's your favourite thing about the rain?" He met my eyes for a moment. I looked back with pure interest and wonder.

"That's a dumb question," he replied, looking back out of the window.

"Well," I started, shifting slightly closer to him. He tried not to notice. "I love the sound. It's so pretty – can something sound pretty? I'm not sure, but if it could, rain would." He turned his gaze slightly right. I sat mesmerised by the rain.

Thunder sounded softly in the distance. He took a deep breath. "Rain is odd. I mean, it's chaotic but peaceful, pleasant but irritating at times. I have never experienced anything quite like rain, and I never wanted to, and then I met you.

"You are rain. So I guess I could say my favourite thing about rain is you." He seemed surprised at what he said and, clearly, based on my wide eyes and dropped jaw, I was too. I could tell he wanted to go back to his room and pretend it never happened.

He moved to get up, but right before he could push himself to his feet, I flung my arms around his neck.

"I love you," I cried. Now it was his turn to be in awe.

Unfiltered

"You-you do?"

"Yes, I do, Nathaniel," I replied, hugging him.

"I love you too," he whispered against my neck. "I mean it was obvious, wasn't it?" he asked.

"Well, not really. Your mood changes more than the weather," I said with a chuckle.

"Yeah, but still I would do anything for you, if you asked me to." He pulled back so he could see my face. "I would walk through hell for you, if you asked," he said, looking deep into my eyes. They shone with love, and for the first time I noticed that his eyes have a little hint of green in them.

"I would do the same for you. I don't know what it is about you, but you're special," I confessed.

"It's like I'm connected to you with an imaginary cord..." he said, furrowing his eyebrows.

"...sometimes it's strong and sometimes it's weak, but it's always there," I finished. "At least we found our way back to each other," I said happily.

"Should we go tell the others the good news?" He sprang to his feet and took my hand gently.

"They won't believe what happened," I said as we closed the door behind us and made our way up to my room.

Turns out Hera and Ash were already talking in our room; we could hear their laughter from outside the door.

Nathaniel opened the door and we walked into the room together, hand in hand. Both of their jaws dropped.

"Hey guys," I said shyly.

"We have a lot to tell you," Nathaniel said.

When we had explained everything that happened, Ash said, "I'm sorry for what happened Astoria, but I told you so." He laughed.

"I knew you would say that! It's fine, you did tell me," I replied, joining him in his laughter.

"I am so happy for you guys! I knew you would find each other again eventually," Hera said, bursting with happiness.

"Not everyone thought so," I muttered.

"Ash?" Nathaniel asked, "What happened?" Something flashed in his eyes that I couldn't quite place – something between caution and anger – before he let it slide. "They sent James for you. We don't know who else is on his side, it could be anyone," he stated.

"You're right, it's not safe for you here, Astoria," Hera said, already working on a plan. "There is only one option," she said, pointing to a very familiar place on the map. "You have to go home, and we'll fight them here in the academy, once and for all," she said, all too confident.

"There's no way I'd let you do that, and you know it! What if I go home and lead them away, and I'll handle them there," I said, knowing that's what I'd do no matter what they said.

"That'll have to wait," I heard someone say, breathing hard as the door opened. A smile spread across his face as he saw me and hugged me tightly.

"I can't believe you're back!" I told Eden.

"I heard what's going on and came here to tell you as fast as I could," he said, concern appeared on his face.

"What is it, Eden?" I asked, getting worried. *Judging by his face, it can't be good.*

"They attacked the castle. Everyone's dead," he said, taking a deep breath.

I stared at him blankly. I was at loss. They had killed everyone I knew, everyone I grew up with. They destroyed my home.

"What about the king?" Nathaniel asked as he took me into his arms.

"He died an honourable death," Eden said, confirming my suspicions. I started sobbing uncontrollably and held onto Nathaniel for dear life.

I was close with my father, but I never got to tell him how much I love him. *He's gone. They killed my family, my parents.*

"Don't, Astoria," Nathaniel whispered as he traced soft circles on my arm. *How did he know what I was thinking? Sometimes I do question if he can read my mind.* I heard a little chuckle behind me; I could tell by the vibration on my skin that it belonged to Nathaniel. I was suddenly aware of how close we were.

"Darling, be aware that the chase is not over. We are not together, we just won't fight each other anymore," he said in a low, husky voice. *Lord, and here I thought I could have some peace.*

"You just can't get enough of it, can you?" I shot back.

"You seem to be the only thing I've had interest in for more than a week. That should say something, love," he replied with a sarcastic smirk I knew all too well.

Funny thing was, I never wanted the chase to end. There was something about it, captivating, not knowing what's next.

Some might say it's toxic, but so what if it is? And what if I need it? The poison running through my veins, making my breath weak?

Someone coughed and I was back in my dorm room, surrounded by the people I care about.

The ones who weren't already dead.

"We need to get back to our plan. Can we please focus for once?" Ash said impatiently. We all sat and stared at the map. It showed many different cities, some of which I had never heard of.

"Why did he attack the castle? He knows that Astoria is here, why would he do that?" Hera questioned Eden.

Because he's an evil monster who doesn't care about anyone but him. He wanted me to feel the pain of losing the ones I care about. He thought it would make me weak. What he didn't know was that it was the opposite. It made me stronger than I was before. Revenge.

"He wanted to hurt me so I would come out and fight him," I said calmly, "and I will."

"No," Eden asserted, and all of them agreed.

They don't have faith in me. They have to trust me. They have no other choice.

"I am not asking for your permission." They shifted away from me, almost as though they were frightened of me. "I'm asking for the best way to do it so I won't die."

All of them seemed to be taken aback; all but Nathaniel.

He sat there, calmly as ever, nothing in his eyes. Coldness and nothing but coldness.

"It's your funeral, not mine," Ash replied breaking the silence. I loved him for that, always trying his best to unite everyone. He would be a great leader someday.

"The best way, as I see it, is that we lead them away from the academy. There are far too many people in danger here," Eden pointed out with a hint of concern.

Finally, someone who thinks logically instead of being selfish.

"It's too dangerous. They know how to fight, his army would be weaker than all of us, and we could kill him here," Ash contended.

"I agree with Ash, Astoria, we can't fight him alone, it would be a suicide mission," Hera said, a concerned look in her eyes.

"That would be selfish!" I said loudly. *I can't believe they are really considering putting that many people in danger. I won't let that happen. No one else's blood must be shed, only his.*

They continued to argue, and before long I wasn't paying attention anymore. Nathaniel was unusually silent, and he seemed to enjoy them arguing.

"Stop fighting, guys!" I yelled, finally having had enough of their drama. "What do you think, Nathaniel?" I asked him, sighing.

"If you ask me," he smirked, "let her lead them to the castle, and we'll see whose blood is shed." I took a sharp breath in. The way he said it, goosebumps run all over my body.

"What if it's going to be her blood that's shed?" I heard Ash exclaim.

Nathaniel stood up and came closer to me. As he brushed past me, he whispered in my ear: "We'll see, won't we, darling?"

I didn't believe him when he said the chase wasn't over. I thought we would tease each other, not be mean. Still, I wasn't surprised, he really never was the same twice. He would always change his behaviour. Suddenly I got the feeling that what we had said this morning wasn't true at all.

Grief

Days later I stood in the graveyard, not far away from the academy. It was unfamiliar, looking down onto the ground and seeing his name on the gravestone.

"Today we gather, to pay our last respects to our beloved King Constantin of Ilimara. May he rest in peace unto eternity," the priest said, addressing the crowd. Everyone wanted to go to the king's funeral; more and more questions arose about what had happened to the queen and why she didn't have a funeral.

I can't *blame them, I would want to know too,* if I was in their position. It would be too dangerous for them to know the truth behind the cover.

"Astoria, it's time," I heard a distant voice say. I stood up, suddenly feeling anxious, like I was about to throw up. There were hundreds of people waiting for my speech, their future queen. I took wobbly steps as I made my way up to the front. When I passed my friends, my gaze lingered on Nathaniel. I longed for him to show a hint of his emotions, to show me that I was not alone in my misery. And there it was, sadness and pride. Confusion hit me as I arrived at the front. Why was he proud?

Stop, Astoria, don't let him ruin your moment.

"Beloved people of all lands, thank you for coming to pay your last respects to the king. He was a good friend, a godfather, a cousin, an uncle, a husband, and a father." I stopped, feeling my voice breaking. I wasn't so sure if I could do this. What *do I even say? Do they knew what happened?* I remembered the advisors telling me that I should tell them that he had a heart attack. I can't just lie to everyone. They deserve to know the truth.

I could tell Nathaniel's eyes were fixed on me. He silently shook his head.

"Dear people, today we mourn not only the loss of the king, but also our queen. They were the best parents that I could've wished for, you know. In my eyes they were normal people. They talked normal, acted normal, and told me bedtime stories like any other parent does. Only when I grew up did I begin to recognise the tiredness in their eyes, constantly worried about their people. They cared more about others than they did about themselves. In a way, that is something I aspire to be. I will honour them with everything I do. It is not only my loss, it is ours, and I would like to share a story with all of you.

"Once, on a summer day when the sun came up, mother woke me. She quietly whispered, "Astoria, come on, be quiet, we'll escape," a huge grin on her face. Suddenly she was young, dynamic, and happy. I hadn't seen her like that a long time, so I played along. Dad was already waiting around the corner. The guards never let us go out alone; we weren't allowed into the woods next to the castle.

"Where are we going, Mom?" I asked her innocently. I was around seven years old and had no clue what was going on.

"We are on a secret mission, sweetheart, we're visiting the forest!" Dad said happily. He brought a huge basket with him, full of delicious food. So, we went out through the back door and left the castle. We walked about twenty minutes before we arrived at the place they had planned. It was stunning, a giant waterfall which shimmered in the summer sun. We went swimming together and ate until we couldn't breathe.

The next moment, Dad jumped up and yelled: "Catch me if you can!" and swam away. I could barely keep up and took a deep breath before jumping into the water beneath me. It was cold, but then I saw him way ahead. "Can't keep up with me can you, sweetie?" he yelled, waiting for me. Mom was laughing and filming us.

"I'll get you, Dad!" I said as I approached him from behind.

"Oh no, the evil sea monster will eat me up!" he exclaimed."

I heard several chuckles in the audience. "I couldn't contain my laughing anymore and almost drowned because of it. When we went back we were questioned about where we were. They lied and said we were asleep the whole time."

Now everyone was laughing. I was smiling, not because I was happy. No. Because that was the only thing I had left of them. Memories.

"Now you all might wonder what happens next. As the king and queen's only biological child, I would be the heir to the throne. And as much as that is an honour for me, I can't accept it." I heard several people gasp in the crowd and people started to murmur. "Quiet!" I yelled over all the people.

Of course they can't *know that I'm* adopted as well, it would be a disaster.

"However, I will take the crown when I'm ready. You deserve the best, that's why I cannot rule right now. My adoptive brother, Eden, will take my place instead until I'm ready to lead you!" I shouted, and people were shocked. I didn't know why I said that, but it was too late now to take it back. I meant it. "He is the person I trust most, and I have faith that he will lead you, my people, well until it's my time to reign!" And with that, I stepped down from the podium and walked away.

I wanted to go far away. *Why couldn't I have the ability to be able to teleport to another place? I know I just went over everyone's head, but that's what's best. I know for a fact that he will lead them better than I could at the moment.*

I have to take care of the other things first before I take the crown. I hope my parents see that too.

I stood far away from the crowd as they started to disperse.

"And here I looked forward to calling you queen," Nathaniel mocked me from behind. I didn't dare turn around; I hoped he would go away. I didn't answer, I was tired, so tired of the responsibility, and I needed to get away.

"Look at me," he said, and something in his voice changed. He wasn't mocking me and there was no sign of sarcasm. It was genuine. He turned me around so I was facing him, but I couldn't look him in the eyes.

He lifted my chin up with his hand and I had to look into his eyes. His mesmerising grey eyes, that sometimes had a hint of green in them. When I looked in his eyes, I didn't see his soul like they always tell you, I just saw a reflection of me. I looked horrible. I need to pull myself together.

"Darling," he said in a low whisper, cupping one of my cheeks with his big hand. "You did the right thing," he assured me, drawing circles on my sensitive skin.

"Did you mean it? What you said yesterday? That you love me?" I asked him seriously.

"Did you?" He deflected the question and took a step back. There it was again, the sarcasm. I was serious, something in me screamed to not trust what he said, but why would he lie? No, he wouldn't *lie*.

"Astoria!" I heard someone yell, and I knew I was in big trouble.

"Hey Eden," I said innocently. "How are you?"

"Don't, Astoria. What were you thinking?! You can't just de-cide something like that over my head!" he yelled at me, furious.

"I am sorry, I am, but I had to do it," I explained.

"God, sometimes I could curse you!" He was frustrated, his hands in his hair, not knowing what to do.

"Look, the advisors will help you, and as soon as I am done with Aaron I will take over, that's a promise," I said, taking a step in his direction.

"Did Mom and Dad approve? Do you think they would?" he asked shakily.

"Of course they would!" I tried to assure him. He nodded and walked away, leaving me alone.

"At least, I hope they would," I whispered, looking up into the sky. I could've sworn I felt a rain drop on my skin, rolling down my cheek in an instant.

I went over to the grave and stood there for a while, silently.

"Hey, Dad," I said sadly, before my voice broke completely. "I will get revenge for what he did, and believe me. I'll do everything in my power to kill him. I just wish you could be here and give me advice.

"It hurts me, deeply, to know that you left without being able to say goodbye. I wish I would've hugged you a little tighter the last time I saw you, that I stayed in your arms for a little longer.

You always told me that you never know when it's going to be the last time you see someone, but I never would've thought that this would ever apply to us. I hope you're in a better place now, united with mom, and that you can be happy. I'll miss you and I'll always remember you, until we meet again." I was sobbing uncontrollably and turned my face away from the grave.

I heard light footsteps approaching, and someone hugged me tight and whispered over and over again that it would be alright. "He would be proud, Astoria, everyone is," Hera said, releasing me from her embrace. It had to be true, I had to believe that in order to move on.

The next days were hard on me, going from press conference to press conference. In the capital, I had just finished the last one. It was exhausting. I always loved the spotlight, but now I couldn't help but wonder if that's really what I wanted.

"They are an even bigger pain in the ass than I am," I heard him say, his all so familiar scent flooded my senses.

"Who would've thought that was possible?" I replied, packing my things up.

Nathaniel did have a thing for timing, always appearing in the worst situations. The way he stood there, leaning on the wall, his head tilted and a smirk plastered on his beautiful face. As much as I hate to admit it, he is beautiful as long as he keeps his mouth shut. I felt his eyes boring into me as I finished packing up.

"Is there something you want?" I asked as I felt myself tense.

"No, I just like to watch you, darling," he said, his smirk growing even bigger.

"You creep," I said, slapping his shoulder as I brushed past him.

I can't wait to take a bath and relax for once. I was in one of the best hotels in town and I finally had time to myself. It was awfully quiet as I walked down the hall, and the sound of my footsteps echoing brought back a long-lost memory.

I was playing in the corridor back home, and I heard voices getting louder and louder. "We can't tell her!" Mom said. By the sound of her voice she has been arguing for some time now.

"Amaris, someday she'll know and then she'll hate you for not telling her, please think logically for once." I recognised Dad's voice, and it made sense that they would be arguing; they did that a lot. But what were they arguing about?

"No! We don't even know for certain that it's the truth, what if it's a lie and we make her life miserable for nothing?" she said, and something slammed against the table.

"She has a right to know where she came from, whether we like it or not," he replied.

"Look at her, she's happy! She's never asked where she came from, so why tell her?" she let out a long sigh.

"It doesn't matter if she asked or not, she still deserves to know the truth! It's selfish not to tell her, she's going to be vulnerable if we don't prepare her," Dad said, frustrated, trying to convince her.

"I can't argue with you, it's for nothing," she said, leaving the office. I saw her tears rolling down her cheek as she walked by, not noticing me.

"Mommy?" I asked sadly.

"Oh," she wiped her tears away quickly before putting on a big bright smile, "hi sweetheart, should we play together?" She took my hand and we walked through the corridors down to the playroom.

Suddenly I became aware of my condition; I had been leaning on a wall for support from the aggressive sobs that escaped my mouth. I tried to cover my mouth with my hand, but it only made it worse. I had a bad headache and felt so exhausted that I could just fall asleep standing. I heard footsteps coming down the hall. Normally I would cover up what just happened, but I couldn't. I heard the steps coming nearer and my vision started to get blurry.

"Astoria?" I heard a voice say before the silhouette sat down next to me. I turned my head to see who it was, only to discover that it wasn't a stranger; no, it was the so-beloved Nathaniel. What is he *of all people* doing here? He can't *see me being weak and vulnerable*.

I quickly brushed my tears away and was just about to stand up as he pulled me back down. I couldn't look into his eyes; it would make me sob even more.

"Look at me." I was surprised by something new in his voice; there was no sarcasm, nothing like the other day in the graveyard. He slightly lifted my chin so my eyes met his.

I searched desperately for a hint of his emotions, something I could cling to, but there was nothing. He had no expression in his face, no emotions. It meant nothing to him, seeing me break down. What did I expect? No, I didn't *expect anything.*

"Sometimes," he paused, and I saw a hint of sadness wash over his features, "Sometimes memories are not as beautiful as they once were. Sometimes they turn out to be our greatest fears, our nightmares, the things that keep us up all night. Whatever you're feeling right now is justified and you have every right to feel that way."

I felt the sobs coming back rapidly and my vision started to get blurry once again. "I-I just feel as if a piece of me is missing and it's not coming back," I wept. I saw in his eyes that he was relaxed, as if he went through things like this all the time.

"Astoria, there is nothing missing from you. You, and you alone, are the only thing you need, everything else is irrelevant. Believe me, it'll fade away slowly, if you let it," he said his hand lingering on my cheek as my tears fell.

I felt sleepy and I only heard snippets of what he said, I rested my head on his lap as he stroked my hair.

"Tell me a story," I murmured. And so he did…

The Little Boy

There was once a well-known man who had a son. The mother died when the little boy was born. She didn't know that her child would have to bear the thought that he killed her for his whole life.

After some time, the boy grew up, and his father trained him to be an assassin for the royal guard. He taught his son to be fearless, even heartless. Some might say he was a bad father, but the boy wouldn't say so. After all he did give him the best gift, the ability to fight. The father meant everything to the little boy; he was the only one he had left.

One night the boy woke up, and nobody was home. He cried out, but nobody came. He was worried what had happened to his father. When the boy searched the house he saw a little note on the fridge:

"Don't come for me."

So he didn't.

He stayed at home, crying all night in worry about his beloved father. He heard voices calling to him, telling him ugly things that could be happening to his father.

Eventually, the little boy fell asleep, until someone burst through the front door and took the little boy with him. The man hadn't been a stranger; it was someone the boy had seen multiple times training with his father. He wouldn't trust him He was so young, he didn't understand what had happened.

The man took care of him – the little boy's father wanted it to be that way. The boy had a good life, but the training didn't stop, and soon after, the boy was almost a weapon, able to kill someone in one swift motion. He could feel his humanity fading.

By day the boy would be heartless, not showing any emotion, but every night he would cry himself to sleep until the voices faded away. The grief, the loss his father left behind was tangible. He would never be the same.

The boy even had a family, a mother and a brother, whom he adored. He was doing alright until one night, it happened all over again.

He woke up in the middle of the night after a nightmare and went looking for someone to comfort him. There was no one there.

He screamed, calling out their names, to no avail. He opened the last door and then the little boy, who wasn't so little anymore, saw them all on the floor in a pool of blood, their throats slit, stabbed multiple times.

The boy screamed, shaking their numb bodies until the man came. He took his hand and they fled to an academy. The man said they would be safe there, and nothing would happen to them.

That night, the boy decided to never let anyone close again, knowing that as soon as someone was too close, they'd die.

Betrayal

I woke up with the sunlight flooding the room in a breathtaking shimmer. I didn't remember how I'd gotten into my bed. The only thing I remembered was Nathaniel telling me a story about a little boy. I tried my best to pay attention to it, but it was hard. My eyelids fluttered open and closed, listening to every detail he told. I felt sorry for the little boy; after all he was only a child.

Maybe my life *isn't that bad. At least I had a loving family and memories no one could take away from me.* I couldn't help but wonder if the story was inspired by someone he knows.

Hell, *I know* it's his story, but I can't feel sorry for him. He has no feelings. But how would I feel if I had a childhood like that? Wouldn't I be selfish and emotionless? Maybe he *isn't that bad after all.*

Checking my phone, I saw a text from my advisor asking me when I wanted to depart to the academy. I texted him that I'd need some time for myself and that I'd text him as soon as I was ready. I had to practice my magic in order to fight Aaron.

I don't know anything about him, but the only thing I need to know is that he is an evil man. He killed countless people and destroyed so many families because of it.

I called Eden earlier and told him that he should try to distract everyone for a while, I needed to be more prepared for the battle. *I'm not ready yet. I need an element of surprise; t*he only useful thing I have, James taught me, so obviously *Aaron knows about it. I'll have to talk to Christopher and ask him to give me more advice.*

I put my training clothes on and went into the gym that the hotel offers. It wasn't as big as I'd expected, but it sure was better than nothing. I wanted to train in combat, even though it isn't easy doing it alone. I made my way to the punching bags, prepped, and went into boxing stance before releasing the first punch. I kept going, throwing punches wildly.

I could feel someone behind me. I tried catching my breath, and as I tried to turn around I felt a drop of hot blood dripping from my throat. It was then when I realised someone held a knife at my throat; by the scent that hovered in the air, I knew exactly who it was.

"Am I such a threat that you have to bring a knife to a fistfight?" I said, knocking the knife out of his grip and turning around.

"I would never underestimate you, darling," he replied, relaxed.

That was his first mistake.

"You shouldn't," I said, and with one swift kick to his leg he was hissing in pain. It took him a few moments before he could react.

His second mistake.

I took the opportunity and started punching him in the ribs and face. He just took it, didn't move. It confused me.

That was my first mistake.

He took advantage of my confusion and stood up and in a matter of seconds he was in front of me, punching me in the stomach. I let out a deep breath and tried to steady myself.

My second mistake.

He went on and punched me right in the nose. My eyes started to water, and I shifted forth and back waiting for him to strike.

He didn't, so I took my chances and I tried punched him in the ribs. He caught my fist and dodged the punch, and the next thing I felt was a strong kick into my diaphragm.

My third mistake.

I couldn't quite catch my breath.

"Deep breaths," he said, "your weakness is that you don't defend yourself the right way." He wasn't even out of breath, not one drop of sweat on his brow. *Does he always have to be so cocky? I hate him, what does he think* he's *doing?* I needed to distract him, he would easily dodge my next attack otherwise.

"The story you told me" "I paused, "It was about you, wasn't it?" I asked, waiting a split second as he hesitated before throwing a punch.

His third mistake.

It had to be one of the strongest I'd ever landed, right into his jaw. He fell back and hissed in pain. "Fuck," he groaned, touching his jaw in pain.

"You did underestimate me, I knew it!" I said proudly as I helped him get on his feet.

"You know I would never, love," he said with his usual smirk.

"Prove it," I said.

We were standing near a wall, and I had already planned out what I'd do. I had picked up the knife earlier in the fight, in the hopes I would to get to use it. He was leaning comfortably against the wall, his breathing relaxed; he had no clue.

"Kill me like he killed your mother," he smirked.

I hadn't expected that response. In all honesty, he was out of line. The memory I tried so hard to avoid came back. Her screaming, him slamming her across the room. Me just standing there, doing nothing but watching my mother die. I feel ashamed that I *just watched. I was weak.*

"You think you can just run that pretty mouth of yours whenever you want?" I asked, trying to hide my anger. I clenched my fists and jaw. He has no right to talk about her, nobody is allowed to talk about my mother. I want to wipe that smirk of his away like Aaron sucked the life out of my mother and so many others. I am done with people underestimating me just because I am a girl. I t*rained hard, I gave everything up so I would be able to fight. He'll feel it soon enough.*

"Make me shut up, then," he said, and in one swift blink I was right in front of him. I could feel his breath on my skin as I held the knife to his throat. Instead of reacting he just smiled. It was the smile he gave when he thought he was in full control. He didn't even flinch when I pressed a little harder, fighting the urge to slice his throat.

"Do it, I dare you, love," he said smiling as he looked down at me, his hair messy, the scar from the fight with James shimmering in the light. And as much as I wanted to do that, I couldn't. I started to shake, the knife trembling in my palm as I slightly stepped back.

I remembered the first thing Cristopher taught me: don't show weakness in front of your opponent, even if you think the fight is over. Nathaniel knew everything I had planned, and I was able to threaten him because he let me do it.

Next thing I knew I slammed into the concrete wall, but my head never met the wall. I heard the knife clatter as it met the hard ground. I was suddenly aware of how close he was; one hand was behind my head, making sure it didn't meet the wall, the other one on my waist. His grip was strong but comfortable.

"Maybe you shouldn't underestimate me, darling," he whispered as his hair tickled my skin. I could almost feel his lips brush mine, but there was nothing I could do. He cornered me. I don't *like him, he is an inhuman monster who was raised to kill people. I* couldn't *love someone like that, ever.* I tried to get out of his grip, and he let me.

I pound my fists into his chest, his eyes dark with pure hatred. "Fight back!" I yell, tears staining my sore cheeks.

"Fight back," and that's when his hands couldn't help but pull me in so close, so vulnerable, and it all happens at once. My lips on his, my back pressed against the wall, my heart desperate for his touch as it betrays everything in me. And in that moment, I hated him. I hated him so much because this was who he made me become.

It was only then when I noticed the sharp pain I felt in my chest. I looked down, my hands covered in blood. I felt short breaths escape my mouth as I looked up into his eyes. I only saw my reflection, knife deep in the chest, blood dripping all over my clothes as I collapsed and fell into his arms. And then there was darkness.

"I was the little boy," I heard him say, as sound faded and I fell.

Two Thrones

I woke up in the middle of a cold, dark room. Where am I? Am I in hell? The air felt thick; it smelled like smoke and death combined. I shivered as a cold breeze went through the room and I realised it wasn't dark, I just couldn't open my eyes. It must *be a giant room,* the way the steps echo. Where am I?

"You weren't supposed to harm her!" I heard an horribly familiar voice call out.

"I had no other choice, believe me, I wouldn't have done it if it wasn't necessary," I heard Nathaniel reply.

"Did you accomplish what I told you?"

"Yes, I did. I have her little heart wrapped around my finger, like you wanted," Nathaniel replied, now speaking in my direction.

"Thank you. Now go, I have some unfinished business," the person commanded.

"No, let me do it, I have some unfinished business as well," he said confidently, but I could feel that he feared the person he was talking to.

"My pleasure," the person said, and I heard footsteps approaching me.

"Open," the person commanded, and instantly my eyes flew open.

I was in a throne room, a black throne room with giant windows and two thrones.

"And so we meet again, child." I looked at the person speaking, somehow both shocked and unsurprised. He was wearing some sort of armour and a crown, and I felt as if I had been thrown back in time. I could feel the anger rising inside me, and knew I wouldn't be able to contain myself much longer.

"You!" I yell at Aaron, whose crooked smile seemed even brighter than before. *I cannot believe it. How did I let myself end up here?* A familiar scent flooded my senses, making me forget everything for a moment.

"Did you like my spy? Did he treat you well?" he asked, amused by my anger.

"You monster! Believe me, I'll kill you as soon as I get the chance," I yelled, but before I could throw myself at him I felt strong arms around my waist. I could feel a heartbeat behind me as he lowered himself to whisper in my ear.

"Don't make it any worse, for your own sake, Astoria," Nathaniel murmured as he traced light circles on my waist. I knew I had no chance against him, but I couldn't just stand there and watch the man who killed so many people.

"You evil bastard! You killed so many innocent people, I hope you'll suffer in hell," I screamed as Nathaniel held me back effortlessly.

"Such a feisty one you got there, Nathaniel," Aaron said, and gave him a grin. "Kill her," was the next thing he said, and I could feel Nathaniel's body tense up immediately.

"You know we can't, did you forget about the ritual?" Nathaniel replied, gripping my waist tighter than before.

"I will never in a million years help you with anything, I'd rather die than help you," I yelled, this time Nathaniel struggled even more holding me back.

"Believe me, my child, by the time we're done, you'll wish you were already dead," Aaron said, amused, and gave a signal to Nathaniel to take me away.

"Don't you think you can get away with this! I'll destroy you–" Nathaniel interrupted me with a hand over my mouth.

"Enough talking, darling," he said as he dragged me out of the throne room.

"Let me go!" I screamed as he pulled me down the corridor. "I can't believe you stabbed me, you traitor!" I continued to scream in his face. *I can't believe he would do that! It makes no sense, since when was he working together with Aaron, and why?*

He lied, all this time, everything was fake. Tears started welling up in my eyes and I heard my voice break.

"Let me go, please," I whispered.

"You know I can't do that, don't make it harder than it already is," he said, and continued to drag me through the corridors. He confused me on purpose, probably so I can't *escape*. *Jokes on him,* I know exactly where I have to *go, he can confuse me all he wants.* There were so much unspoken between us, and I could feel the tension.

We arrived at two doors, both black. Everything here was black. *I guess they really like that colour.*

"That's your room," was the only thing he said before pushing me in and closing the door, leaving me alone. The room was beautiful. Everything was black except the bed, which was sage green and covered with silk sheets. There were windows everywhere; one wall was completely covered with windows. You would expect the sun to consume a room like that, but for the first time since I got here I saw where I was. I walked over to the windows, only to realise that I had my own balcony. At least I have a nice room.

I stepped out onto the balcony and a light breeze brushed over my skin. I shivered at the view beneath. It looked as if a storm was coming; the clouds were pitch black, the city underneath was black. It looked majestic, but where was I? I looked for a way to escape, but it was impossible. The balcony was far too high for me to jump. I went back in and laid down on the bed.

I can't believe it. Why would Nathaniel do this? This can't be real, this has to be another nightmare. There is no way Nathaniel would do that. I trusted him. He stabbed me as if it meant nothing to him. I will kill him, he can count on that.

I heard a knock on my door and sat up on my bed. A woman entered my room. She looked like a dark queen – *I guess people here just give off those vibes.* Her dark skin shimmered, her black hair in a ponytail.

"The king wants you to wear a dress for tonight, so I've brought you one," she said, her voice surprisingly kind. *I take it she's a maid.*

"King? Where am I?" I asked her curiously.

"You don't know? We're in the shadow realm, the kingdom of Onyx, where King Aaron reigns," she said, smiling as she laid the dress softly on the bed.

"Why would you support such a cruel person? He killed hundreds of innocent people!" I said heatedly. *Why would people follow Aaron? Don't they know what kind of person he is?*

She looked surprised at first, but then her expression changed – to fear. "There is nothing we can do, we have no choice," she admitted quietly, as though she was afraid that someone might hear us.

You always have a choice. They could ask for *help,* or overthrow him. It doesn't *make sense, why would they let someone rule whom* they're *scared of?* "Why don't you ask for help?" I asked. *There must be someone that would help them.*

"Do you know anything about us?" she asked me, irritated.

I didn't even know this place existed, and I had no clue that Aaron was a king.

I can't show weakness, I have to act as if I know everything. I hate when people underestimate me, they should think I know exactly what's going on. "Of course I know," I lied.

She looked sceptical. I couldn't quite name her expression, but I would say she didn't suspect anything yet. "Well then you should know that everyone hates us. The light realm and the shadow realm are mortal enemies, they wish death on us. The human realm, where you come from, doesn't know that we exist, so you see the problem," she explained.

Of course everyone hates them, they are evil. Just look at their king, what kind of people do you expect to follow him? I looked at the maid. *Maybe I was wrong. Maybe the people really don't have a choice.*

"Get ready, the prince will pick you up in an hour," she said, opening the door. Prince? Who's the prince? I stopped her before she could leave.

"What's your name?" I asked, and I could see her face light up a little.

"I'm Alyssa," she said.

"It was nice meeting you, I'm Astoria," I said, and let her go.

"Oh, I know," she said, and the door closed.

How did I end up in this misery? I *mean, I* know d*amn well how,* but how could I let that happen? They must be worried about me back home. I'm *sure Ash and Hera will find me.*

They'll *know that* something's *off when they find out* Nathaniel and I *are missing. Why did no one tell me that there were different realms? There's no way I can escape, I* don't *even know how I got here. Maybe if I play along, I'll get some insider information that'll help me escape.*

My eyes landed on the beautiful gown on my bed. It was a black gown with little embellishments on it. The bodice was an almost see-through corset, and it fit me perfectly. The slit on the leg was just enough to see my leg. When I looked into the mirror I saw my reflection for the first time since I got here. I looked like the life had been sucked out of me, like the kiss of death. My skin was pale, and with my black hair and red lips I even looked like Snow White. Thank god I'm used to wearing high heels, I thought when I saw them. They were as beautiful as the dress and matched and fit all too perfectly. *Did they take my measurements?*

Imagining what they did when I was unconscious was enough to make me shiver. I knew I would need some kind of weapon, so I looked around the room, but there was nothing that I could use.

"If you wanted one of my knives you could've just asked," I heard Nathaniel say behind me.

I turned around, startled. "Do you walk into strangers' rooms without knocking all the time?" I asked, mocking him.

"I definitely wouldn't call us strangers, darling," he said, leaning on the door.

"I don't know who you are, and apparently I never did, so yes, we are complete strangers," I said, trying to not sound hurt.

"I suppose you're right. The only difference is that I know everything about you, and you don't know anything about me," he replied in a husky voice as his head tilted to the side.

He's trying to provoke me, but he won't. No, what he says and does doesn't affect me in any way. But he was right, I knew nothing about him, and he knew everything about me. I could feel him staring.

"Is there something you want? I got told that the prince would pick me up, I bet he's more charming than you are," I said as I pushed him out of the room.

"I'm sure he is," was the last thing I heard before I shut the door in his face. I needed to punch something, I was so angry. I can't *believe* he's *still here*. Didn't *he finish his job?*

I heard a knock on my door. *Finally. I can't wait to get out of here and see where I am.* I opened the door to see Nathaniel once again. I let out a deep sigh, he was really testing my patience. "I'm here to escort Astoria to the king," Nathaniel said with a charming smile.

"You think you're funny, don't you? Next time I see you I'll kill you with your own knife," I said as charmingly as I could. He thinks this is a joke. I really hope the prince is more enjoyable company than he is. *Honestly,* the bar is on the ground, there's *not much he could do wrong.*

I saw some maids walking past us, and one of them bumped right into Nathaniel. She was lucky that he caught her just in time.

"Oh my god, my deepest apologies, your highness!" the women said, blushing.

"Don't worry, m'lady," Nathaniel said with a wink.

It hit me. *No, there is absolutely no way in hell Nathaniel is the prince of Onyx.*

"Now, what are you waiting for?" he said smirking.

"There is no way that's true." I stated the obvious. There were a lot of things I could believe, but Nathaniel being a prince wasn't one of them. But when I looked at him, there was no smirk, no smile. This was serious. No. That would make him − "You're Aaron's son?" I was almost speechless. To my surprise, he didn't look amused; he almost looked sad. He quickly covered his emotions with a smirk.

"You don't have to call me 'your highness'," he replied.

Guest of Honour

I was in a different realm, somewhere I didn't know anything about. And the prince of the realm turned out to be the one who stabbed me. *I suppose that isn't a surprise. I can't believe I kissed the prince of the shadow realm! I trusted him with everything. I am helpless, Aaron knows everything about me. There is nothing I could do that he wouldn't see coming. I'm screwed.*

The betrayal must have been written all over my face. "Don't look at me like that, love, it's not personal," he said, attempting to sound reassuring. *What was it if not personal? He played me like a violin.* I stared at him in disbelief as I began to realise what all of that actually meant.

"All this time I thought you were a good guy, when in reality you're the worst of them all," I said, and this time I couldn't help showing how hurt I was. My voice betrayed me, and a sob escaped my mouth. "You're right, I don't know anything about you," I said, and shut the door.

How could that be possible? No, his feelings must have been real, there is no way he faked all of it. I thought his father died, was that a lie? When I think about it, it all makes sense.

He was trained to be a weapon, that's what he was prepared for his whole life. He *really fooled everyone, especially me.* My vision started to go blurry. *No, I won't cry because of him. His betrayal means nothing to me, he means nothing to me. He never did.* I tried keeping the tears from falling and opened the door.

He was gone.

This was my opportunity to have a good look at the castle. I made my way through the long halls. The walls were all black, and I started to see the beauty in it. Suddenly I heard voices down the hall, so I slipped into a room to listen.

"I heard he needs her for the Vladium, that's why she's still alive," I heard one say.

"He'll probably kill her right after she uses it to destroy the light realm," the other one replied. Wait, to destroy the *light realm? Why would I help him with that?* The voices faded, and for the first time I looked around. I was in an office. There were books that looked older than the world. Suddenly I saw a little knife on the desk.

Bingo!

I quickly grabbed it and hid it in one of my sleeves. *Thank god this dress was made like that.* I stepped into the corridor and made my way towards the noise.

I took multiple staircases before I finally saw where the noises came from. There were people all over the place, mingling and having fun with each other.

I tried to stay hidden, but someone caught my eye in the crowd. Aaron's eyes lit up as he saw me on the steps.

"Everyone, meet the guest of honour, Astoria!" he yelled, raising his glass. So much *for staying hidden. What if I play along with it? Then I'll betray them just like they did me.* A smile appeared on my face at the thought of their faces when they realised I'd betrayed them. I walked down the stairs and smiled gracefully at the guests.

"She's the saviour of us all, please show her some respect!" he yelled once again as I approached him. "Hello dear, I'm grateful that you dressed the part. This ball is for you, I hope you like it," he said, smiling. As he brushed past me, he gripped my arm. "Don't do anything stupid, you'll just make it worse for yourself," he said in a low growl, before making his way over to some guests.

Great, what am I supposed to do now? I have to find a way to slip away from the crowd so I can find a way out of that castle. Should I go to the bathroom? No, there could be other people there. I wandered around the gigantic room. There were windows as tall as the ceiling; it was breath-taking. I didn't expect to find such beauty in a place like that.

I heard music start playing. That was my chance. Everyone would be busy, and nobody would notice if I wasn't present, at least I hoped so.

I started walking to the corner of the room and left the ballroom. Nobody seemed to notice. There was a door at the end of the corridor labeled 'laboratory.' I opened the door without hesitation and was surprised to find nothing cruel. However, there were a bunch of bottles on the shelves. You could kill thousands of people with the amount of poison there is *in here*. There were all sorts of poisons; some could kill you, even make you bleed internally. I knew that only one person would notice right away that I was gone.

Nathaniel.

I have to do something to knock him out, maybe even kill him. There's nothing I'd rather do. He betrayed me. He lied all this time and used it to get his way with his father. He lied to all of us. I browsed through the bottles, but I had no knowledge of poisons. *I can't risk making a mistake. I don't think I have to be worried about time, I didn't see Nathaniel at the ball.* Something caught my eye as I searched the shelves. It was a small bottle, it looked blue, almost violet. I didn't know what it was but it was engraved on the bottle that it was the kiss of the death. *How fortunate for me, I only need to know how it affects people.*

I took the bottle, and heard people starting to search for me. I slipped it under my dress just before the door opened.

Instead of Nathaniel, a beautiful woman entered the room. She had red hair and blue eyes, and she was about my age. Her red dress complemented her hair perfectly. "Ah, so I finally meet the famous Astoria, what a pleasure," she said, her voice dripping with sarcasm.

"I'm sorry, I needed to go to the bathroom but I ended up here," I lied, making my way over to the door.

"Come on, I'll show you," she said, and we left the laboratory. "Do you like it here?" she asked me.

"It's all new to me. It's different but it has its own beauty," I said, admiring the details in the corridor. I couldn't help but feel alarmed by her presence, she glowed with power. Something about her intrigued me. She reminded me of someone, I just couldn't say who.

"Who are you, by the way?" I asked the stranger.

"I'm Raven, Princess Raven," she said. That made sense.

"You're Nathaniel's sister?" I asked her as we stepped into the bathroom.

"Sadly, I am. He is a real pain in the ass, isn't he?" she asked, annoyed.

"Oh, tell me about it!" I replied. I heard her humming while I was in the stall.

"He told me a lot about you, Nathaniel," she said as I walked out of the door. Of course he did, to give you intel on me. "Where are you from?" she asked as I washed my hands.

"You already know everything about me, stop pretending that you don't," I said. I'm done with people thinking they can fool me.

"You're right," she chuckled.

As I went to leave, she grabbed my shoulder and starred into the depths of my soul. "If you try anything to harm my family or escape, I'll cut your head off," she said, and let me go.

Something about her didn't make sense. I never knew Nathaniel actually had a sister, there were only two thrones. Why would there only be two thrones if she was the princess as well? I went back into the ballroom. Looks like I just made it in time to dance.

My gaze landed on Nathaniel. He was leaning on the wall, his eyes tired as he watched the couples dance. I can't believe that boy betrayed me. I don't think I'll ever fully realise it. I can't get my head around the fact that everything was a lie. It can't be. But then, he was trained for that.

He seemed to tense up when his father approached him. His smile faded, his jaw clenched. He was scared of Aaron, I could see it. They both looked over at me as they talked, although I couldn't hear them. When Aaron left, Nathaniel slumped back against the wall once again, letting out a deep breath. Should I go and talk to him? No, he would just lie again like he did before. I turned away, not knowing what to do.

"Would you do me the honour of dancing with me, Queen Astoria?" I turned around and saw Nathaniel grinning sheepishly at me. He looked as handsome as ever as he held his hand out.

"Only if you stop calling me that, Prince Nathaniel," I replied, and took his hand.

His hand was warm, and he had a comfortable grip as he lead me onto the dance floor. A slow song started playing and I tried my best to keep my distance from him. I felt the cold blade of the knife against the skin of my arm and remembered my plan. I closed my eyes and my imagination betrayed me. What if nothing happened and it was just Nathaniel and me? What if it was real? A teardrop rolled down my cheek and I quickly brushed it away.

"Are you alright?" he asked, his chin resting against the top of my head.

"You have the answer to that question yourself," I replied. I didn't care if my voice trembled.

"You can stab me if it makes you feel better," he whispered.

"You can count on that," I snorted.

"I can't wait, darling," he said, and suddenly I was aware of how close we actually were. I could feel his heartbeat and I'm pretty sure he could hear mine. "But let me warn you, don't make the same mistake again. Don't underestimate me," he said.

God, he's full of himself. The hardest thing to admit was that he was right, I did underestimate him. I heard the song start to end, and I slowly released myself from his embrace.

"I feel tired. I want to go to sleep," I told him.

"Alright," he said and hooked my arm in his. As we passed the guests I heard some of them whispering.

"What are you doing?" I whispered angrily. We took the staircases to the top floor, where my room was. "Can you leave me alone for once, please?" I asked, annoyed, as I slapped his hand away.

"I was assigned to watch over you," he said, amused. *Out of all people in this palace, I got the most annoying one.*

"Where would I even go, Nathaniel? I'm trapped here, and I don't know the way out!" I yelled frustrated. *It's not like I have a choice. If* I knew how to leave, I would've *done that a long time ago.* He didn't say anything, but he stopped and looked at me. "You put me in this misery, this is your fault!" I yelled and pointed my finger at him. "How could you?!" I was interrupted as he captured my hand, pulling me awfully close.

"Listen here, love, if not for me you would be dead now, so please be grateful for once. I am trying my best to keep you alive, but if you don't stop I won't be able to help you," he said loudly, even though I was right up in his face. I could smell his minty breath as he spoke. Maybe not all hope is lost, maybe not everything was a lie. His familiar scent was comforting; he was the only thing I knew.

Suddenly I started sobbing, I couldn't control it anymore, it just came out of me.

They were light sobs but when he held my head and held me even tighter, it was hard to not break down completely. How did we end up here? Both feeling helpless but trying to protect each other.

"I won't let anything happen to you." His words were a promise, I knew that. We walked in pure silence and before he could close the door I stopped.

"Can you please not lock the door?" I asked him in fear.

I had told him back in the day that I was often locked up by the staff at the palace. I would have terrible nightmares, demons that were coming for me, but I couldn't do anything. They did that until I was fifteen, and I never recovered from it.

"I won't," he said and closed the door.

Sakra

I woke up when I heard noises from outside. I was sleepy even though I got more than enough sleep. I put on my night gown and stepped onto the balcony. I could see people on the streets; it looked like they were celebrating. I found it intriguing. Even in a sad and cruel place like that, they still find a way to enjoy life and celebrate. A sudden wave of sadness came over me. I miss my friends. I miss my family. I miss everything I've *ever known*. *I miss the feeling of the sun on my skin.*

"It's beautiful, isn't it?" I whirled and threw the knife at the unknown person, only to see Nathaniel catching the knife effortlessly. "Good throw," he said, impressed, as he looked at the knife. He came over to me and handed it back to me.

Why would he just give me the knife without questioning it? "What are they celebrating?" I asked him, watching the people dance with each other.

"It's the festival of Sakra," he replied. "She was a legend, the saviour of the shadows, kind of like you," he continued on.

"That's what I don't understand, why does your father need me?" It still felt weird calling Aaron Nathaniel's father.

"There is a blade, Vladium, which has the power to destroy a whole realm. My father wants it to destroy the light realm," he explained.

"What role do I play in this scenario?" I asked. It was no surprise that he wanted to destroy the light realm, I just didn't know what that had to do with me.

"I don't know, that's what I'm trying to find out," he said, a hint of frustration showing on his face.

"Do you want to go?" he asked, pointing down at the celebrations in the city. Do they *trust me enough to let me go into the city? I would love to see the people here,* and it couldn't *hurt to get out of this place for once.* Was this another one of his plans, or was it genuine this time? It doesn*'t matter, this could be the perfect opportunity to escape. He*'s *alone,* and if I plan it right, I should be able to outrun *him.*

"You already know the answer," I said, grinning, and I dressed myself. I didn't care if he was there, as long as he shuts his mouth and stares out of *the balcony, I should be fine.* I chose a white dress, a little shorter than knee-length, then took a leather blazer that was in the closet and threw it over the top. I knew it would be better if I wore sneakers, so I took a pair of white ones and the knife Nathaniel handed me, hiding it between my shoulder blades. This should be fun. Two can play this game.

"Let's go," I said, smiling, and waited for him to leave the room.

Instead of covering my eyes or making sure I didn't know where the exit was, he went straight towards it; by the security that was there, I knew I would have no chance of escaping that way. He just smiled and he took my hand, and we ran.

I had no clue what was going on. *Why would they follow us? I thought it was alright, did he betray his father?*

"Come on!" he yelled, and dragged me through the garden that lay in front of the castle. We took several stairs and suddenly we were in the middle of the festival. I was out of breath and tried to catch my breath.

"That was fun," I laughed. *Finally, some adrenaline.*

"It won't be when we get back," he said seriously, but with a grin on his face.

It was stunning: the city wasn't all black, instead the houses were decorated with colourful flags and lanterns. It was breathtaking; everyone was dancing and cheering. I hadn't seen anything like it before. Children were playing and adults were dancing together. The valley was filled with an amazing scent, and I heard my stomach growl. I'm sure even Nathaniel could hear it over the loud noise.

"Come on, I bet you're hungry," he said, and took my hand.

I held onto his arm tightly, overwhelmed by all the people.

Some time later we arrived at a food truck, and it smelled delicious. Nathaniel came back with a plate full of chips and chicken. The second he put the plate down I dug in. It was as delicious as it smelled.

"This is one of the best things I've ever had," I said while munching away. Nathaniel sat across from me, but he hadn't been eating that much.

"It's one of our specialties. You should enjoy, we eat it once a year," he said, trying to force a smile. Something was up, I knew it. The way he acted; he didn't even eat.

"Look Nathaniel, I might not know the real you, but I know when something's wrong, what is it?" I asked him seriously, looking directly into his eyes.

"Like you said, you don't know the real me. This is how I am, nothing's up," he replied coldly. That must be a lie, but... *how would I know something's off when I don't even know him?* I remembered the plan. I have to *distract him and then run off. I don't know where to go,* but everywhere is better than in the castle with Aaron.

"Can you tell me the story of Sakra?" I asked cautiously. I knew that I would get some new information; he did compare me to her.

"Thousands of years ago, when the war broke out between the light and shadow realms, there was a woman who was special and possessed a special blade.

She knew for certain that this blade could end the war once and for all, if she destroyed one of the realms. She couldn't do it: she grew up in the light realm, and spent her days here, in the shadow realm. The decision was too hard for her, the power too much. She couldn't bear seeing one of them suffer. One night she went into the mountains and never came back.

It's said that she killed herself with the Vladium; she sacrificed herself for the sake of both realms. That's why we celebrate her every year." As he told me the story, his eyes lit up and whenever something interesting came up he got excited.

"But she didn't stop the war?" I asked. *She could've ended the war and they could've lived happily ever after.*

"If she would've used the Vladium, we would all be dead, there would be no one left," he explained.

Now I get it, they compared me to her because I would have to do the same *thing* she did. I would have to end one of the realms, and they want to make sure it *isn't their realm that gets destroyed. It makes sense, they're only trying to survive. It was true, not everyone here is bad.* The weight on my shoulders just doubled; I could understand Sakra's decision.

We made our way through the valleys; it was truly beautiful, but the only thing that was on my mind was my plan to escape. I would need a distraction. No, why am I even *bothering trying to distract him, he would see right through it. I need another plan. Maybe he would let me* go. *Maybe not all hope is lost for him.*

"Nathaniel," I grabbed his hand and he stopped. He looked me in the eyes, and I saw the same eyes which told me that they love me, which were there for me. *There has to be at least a little part in him that feels the hurt I'm in.*

"You have to let me go," I said quietly. I was aware that we were alone in the valley; nobody could see us.

"I can't do that, Astoria," he said, and for the first time in days I could see that the situation was hurting him as much as it hurt me.

"Please, Nathaniel, you know I won't do what they're asking me to do, I can't," I pleaded, voice trembling.

"Don't you understand? You have no choice, you don't know where to go!" he yelled, and I cornered him against the wall.

"Please Nathaniel, you need to let me go, if there is even a small part in you that cares for me, you have to let me go," I said pleadingly.

"Darling, there is no part in me that cares about you. They need you, that's all you are," he said, not looking me in the eyes. I took the dagger from between my shoulder blades and held it to his throat.

"At least look me in the eyes when you lie to me!" I yelled, getting awfully close to his face.

"It was all a game, everything," he snorted as he looked me straight in the eyes. And I could see it. He meant every single word of it.

"Remember, you left me no other choice," he said, and I fell into darkness once again.

Forgiveness

I heard keys jingle as my eyes flew open.

"Thank you, son," I heard Aaron say from above me. We were in the throne room. *Talk about* déjà vu. Aaron and Nathaniel sat on their thrones, Raven standing beside them. *I'll* never understand why she doesn't get her own throne.

"Now, now, look at you, my child," Aaron chided, approaching me. What is he going to do? He can't kill me, there *is nothing he could do to hurt me.* I wanted to speak, but nothing came out of my mouth. What is going on? Why can't I speak?

"Funny, right? I can make you shut up whenever I want. Isn't that brilliant?" Aaron jeered, taking my chin so I had to look at him. "My dear, you're not making it easy. You're going to be a hero! Everyone will cheer your name," he continued. "Speak," Aaron commanded.

"I'd rather die than help you evil people!" I screamed. To my surprise, they could actually hear me. I could see Nathaniel out of the corner of my eye, pinching the bridge of his nose and sighing. I can't *believe he's* letting this *happen to me. On* second thought, I shouldn't *be surprised, he is the prince of the shadow realm. He was raised to be heartless.* Raven stared at me in anger. I didn't like her at all.

"You have no choice, it's useless! Nobody's coming to save you, you don't even know how to leave the realm, why do you even bother trying?" he asked, chuckling.

"Maybe I do know how to escape," I lied, grinning at him.

I could see his jaw clench; I hit his sweet spot. "Take her away, I can't promise I won't harm her if I see her any longer," he said loudly and Nathaniel stood up.

"Father," Raven said and motioned towards the guards.

Nathaniel took me and dragged me towards the door. "There is nothing you can do, you can't hurt me!" I said, laughing.

"Bring her in," Aaron commanded the guards, and the door opened. It was Alyssa. "Maybe I can't hurt you, but I certainly can hurt the ones you care about," he said cruelly, and laughed.

"Leave her alone, you monster!" I called out, and tried to throw myself at him. Nathaniel held me back without struggle and crushed me against his chest. The guard shoved her onto the cold ground and took out a whip.

"Ten," Aaron commanded, and Alyssa looked at me. She looked terrified.

"No! Stop, please!" I screamed, and tried to escape Nathaniel's grip.

"Close your eyes," Nathaniel whispered as he held me tight, but I heard her screams. They reminded me of the screams my mother gave the night she died.

"Stop!" I yelled, crying.

"Ten," the guard said, and Alyssa was laying on the ground, screaming.

"I hope you learned your lesson, for the sake of your maid," Aaron said coldly, and Nathaniel took me away.

We were standing in the hallway, but I didn't move. I was angry and hurt. *She was innocent! They should've* hurt me instead. "This is your fault! All of it!" I screamed at Nathaniel, punching his chest desperately.

"I told you to stop! This is your fault, you shouldn't have tried to run away!" he said, hushed.

"Take me to her, right now!" I screamed, I needed to see her and make sure she was okay. *This was my fault. She had to suffer because of me.* He looked as if he weighed the options he had and then he walked away in silence. I followed him and he quietly opened a door.

"Hurry, you don't have much time," he said and closed the door behind me.

There were multiple beds in a row, but her bed was the only one which was occupied. I made my way to her bed and quietly sat next to her. She was lying on her stomach. *I can't begin to imagine the pain she must be in.*

"Alyssa, I'm so terribly sorry, this is my fault," I said, sobbing. I really liked her, we spent a lot of time together.

"You're right, we have to run away, we can't let Aaron rule any longer," she gasped.

"I know, but you have to rest, I have to wait until I have a better plan, we can't trust Nathaniel. I have to find a better way to get out, give me some time," I explained, holding her hand.

"Astoria, I'm scared, what if they do it again?" she sobbed.

"I won't let anything happen to you, I promise," I said, and gave her hand a squeeze. I heard the door open and Nathaniel motioned for me to get out. "Be strong, everything will be alright," I said to her before leaving.

We walked in silence to my room; I had nothing left to say to him. I opened the door and closed it right away. l couldn't believe he let them do that. Maybe I have to face the truth that he's *evil and as cruel as his father. I have to stop being surprised when something like that happens.*

Weeks passed and nobody came to get me. I wandered through the castle and sometimes I was even allowed to go out into the city – with Nathaniel watching my every step, of course. I never said a word to him. It turned out they were waiting for the hunters to find the Vladium, until then there was nothing much I can do. Apart from plotting my escape of course. This family is fucked up, nobody cares about anyone, I'm *sure they would all kill each other if they could.* I found some beautiful spots in the castle; there was even a gallery with beautiful paintings. I found myself wandering through it multiple times. Some of the paintings felt familiar – I couldn't quite place what it was, but I felt connected to them.

"Beautiful, aren't they?" I heard Raven's voice approaching me.

"The artist is very talented, each painting tells its own story," I said, impressed. She seemed distracted. She had tried to reach out to me several times, but I never wanted to talk because she scared me. *I don't trust her.*

"Astoria…" She sounded worried. She sat down and buried her face in her palms.

"Is everything alright?" I asked and sat down next to her.

"It's Nathaniel, he's not the same. I haven't seen him in days, and his mother's birthday is just around the corner. I'm scared that it's affecting him more than I suspected," she told me, scared. *He never talked about his mother, he told me she died early, maybe that was a lie?*

"How did she die?" I asked quietly.

"She died giving birth to Nathaniel, he never got to know her. He feels guilty, he thinks he killed her," she explained. *At least that's one thing he didn't lie about.* Truth was I hadn't seen him either, I thought maybe it had gotten boring watching over me and he decided to leave me. Maybe I was wrong.

"I thought you didn't care about each other?" I asked sceptically. I thought they hated each other, they barely spoke.

"Why did my father choose Alyssa, out of all the people he could've tortured?" she asked, and the realisation hit me. They acted like they didn't care for each other so that their father couldn't use their weakness against them. They did it to protect each other.

"I will find him, Raven," I assured her.

"I know I wasn't kind to you in the past, but I never wanted to hurt you, our father is too strong," she explained genuinely. I didn't know what to say, so I stood up and left the gallery.

I searched the whole palace, but found no trace of him. I went outside, the cold breeze softly brushing over my skin, making me shiver. I searched the whole garden and had almost given up when I spotted him at the edge of the garden, looking over the city.

"Nathaniel!" I let out a relieved scream. He didn't react. As I approached him I saw multiple bottles of alcohol on the ground, all empty.

"Go away," he murmured.

I silently sat down next to him, the grass damp from the fog. He took the bottle and started to drink again, almost chugging the whole bottle. I slapped the bottle out of his grip, and it took him several seconds to look at me in disbelief.

"Stop it! Snap out of it, Nathaniel," I said loudly. He slumped back against the tree and closed his eyes.

"Why do you care about me? I never cared about you! I am a monster, why are you helping me?" he asked, confused.

"You may have never cared about me, but I always cared about you, and by the way, I'm not a monster," I said, sitting right next to him now.

"I wish I met her," he whispered, looking down at the city. It was silent. I assumed that the realisation hit them that their fate was in my hands.

"I know," I whispered, and suddenly his head was in my lap. He softly looked up and met my eyes.

"I'm sorry he killed your mother, nobody deserves that," he whispered. *I'm sure that's just the alcohol talking. Nothing he's saying is the truth, he's drunk.* We sat there in silence for a bit before he started sobbing. At first I thought I misheard something, but then I saw a tear escape his eyes.

"Even if you never met your mother, I see her in you, the kindness, it's there, I saw it," I assured him wiping his hair out of his face.

"But you still won't be able to forgive me, ever?" he asked, insecure. I didn't know what I should answer. That was definitely the alcohol talking. He wouldn't remember anything I told him.

"No, I'll never be able to forgive you, you have to forgive yourself first," I whispered into the cold evening air.

Maybe not all villains are bad, we just don't want to hear their story. Maybe if we did, we'd understand them.

Sacrifice

Seeing Nathaniel that vulnerable made me question if he was really a bad person. He had no choice. No, you always have a choice, always. It was the next morning, and I hadn't heard anything from him. I made my way to his room and knocked on the door. He opened the door, his chest bare and his skin covered in paint.

"What do you want?" he asked, annoyed.

I tried to ignore the fact that he was almost naked, and couldn't believe my eyes when I saw what he was painting. "I didn't know you could draw," I mocked him, and went straight past him.

"What do you want, Astoria?" he asked again, closing the door.

"I wanted to talk about last night," I said, sitting down on his bed. His room was big and black, no surprises there. He had windows behind his bed just like I did. Our rooms were pretty similar, except that he got to draw.

"I was drunk, it's not like I can remember anything," he said, and threw on a shirt. That was probably true. *I was right, he didn't mean anything he said yesterday.* My eyes landed on the painting: a girl, blade deep in her chest. It told its own story. I couldn't help but notice the resemblance she had to me.

"Since when do you paint?" I asked him, walking over to the painting.

"I'm just doing it to get my mind off the situation, it helps me cope," he said, and sat down next to me.

"Is that…" I stopped, not knowing if I should ask. "Am I the girl?" I asked cautiously. *He'll probably deflect the question and close himself up again.*

"No, that's Sakra, the way they described her; she stabbed herself at the top of the mountain," he replied. It was shocking, she did look like me.

"So you're drawing me as well," I said. *It will be me as soon as I get the chance. My destiny may be the same as Sakra's. Maybe we were meant to sacrifice ourselves.*

He looked at me, stunned. "I won't let you do it, you know that," he said gently. He wasn't angry or mad; it seemed as if he was worried.

"You won't be able to stop me. I don't have a choice, it's my destiny," I said, standing up.

"You always have a choice, remember? You're the one always talking about how you always have a choice, and now? You just surrender? I thought more of you, I really did," he said, standing up as well.

How dare he compare us? He had a choice, I don't. "You leave me no choice, either I kill myself or I have to destroy a whole realm! There is no choice, I won't let innocent people die!" I said, getting angrier.

I wouldn't be able to live with myself, knowing that thousands of people died because of me, even though it could've been stopped. *I can understand Sakra, I can understand why she had to do what she did. I may not be able to stop the war, but I can stop the end of a realm.*

He took a step back as if the words that left my mouth hurt him. They should, it's his fault after all. It's his fault that I landed here in the first place.

"Just know that when I kill myself, it's going to be your fault, and you're the one who has to live with that," I said, and left the room in a hurry.

I ran to my room and found Alyssa. She was startled as I came in in a rush. "We don't have much time anymore, I told Nathaniel that I would kill myself, it's only a matter of time before they lock me up," I said in a hurry.

"Astoria, breathe. I heard the guards talking, they found the Vladium. It's too late," she said, but I was already in my mind.

"No, it's not too late, Alyssa, the sword was destroyed, they have to fix it first. I just need a distraction," I said, trying to convince her.

"Are you sure, Astoria? It's too risky, they will be alerted and start to watch you more," she said. She wasn't convinced anymore. *I can't just leave her here, she* doesn't *deserve a life like that.* "And what would you do if you succeed? You don't know how to go to another realm!" she reasoned. She was right, but I had to try. *It's better than giving up.*

"I won't force you to come with me, but I will go, I can't stay here," I said and started packing my things.

"Wait, Astoria, please, let's just think," she said, stopping me.

"I have to go, they'll lock me up, I know it!" I said, continuing to pack my things.

"Just wait until tomorrow evening! They're throwing a ball, we can escape then without anyone knowing," she assured me.

She's right, it would be too obvious to run away now. I have to wait until everyone is distracted. "All right, but do you have a plan to escape?"

"There's a staff exit, it leads to a tunnel that ends at the edge of the city, once we're there we'll figure out how to continue," she said. It was a good plan, especially because of the tunnel.

"But I have to attend the ball, where are we going to meet?" I asked her. *I wish she could come to the ball with me, it's a shame that they aren't allowed to.*

"We'll meet up in the gallery, the tunnel is there, nobody knows about it. You just have to slip away from the crowd without anyone noticing," she said. This plan will be successful. It has to be. By the way Alyssa looked at me, I knew that she wasn't sure if she did the right thing.

"Hey, if you don't want to come with me, that's fine," I said genuinely.

"I know, but Astoria, you can't go alone, it's too dangerous," she said with conviction. "You just have to find a way to distract Nathaniel." I knew I had to; I had wanted to kill him a long time ago. I would have to prepare myself for the scenario that I had to kill him. After all, what he did was even worse. I remembered the poison I picked up on the first night I was here.

"Do you know what the poison 'kiss of death' causes?" I asked her, examining the little bottle. She came over and had a look at it.

"Yes, I think so, it was used to poison people who you kiss, it poisons the person immediately and knocks them unconscious for hours. You put it onto your lips and the person you kiss will be poisoned," she said.

That's brilliant! I can use that on Nathaniel without killing him. I just have to make him kiss me, I don't think that will be a problem.

"Will you be able to handle it?" she asked me before leaving.

"It will be the least of our problems," I said, and she left. I'm sure it'll work. I stepped onto the balcony. It was evening now. I thought about the time I had spent here. It wasn't *all bad. I had fun,* and even if there were painful moments, I met people and got to know many things about them. You'd think *they were bad if someone told you about a shadow realm, but they aren't.*

I miss home though. I miss being at the academy, surrounded by my friends. I would give everything to go back to when I didn't know the painful truth.

Ash will kill Nathaniel as soon as he gets to know who he actually is. And even if Nathaniel is bad, my heart is still aching for him. My heart an*d brain are at war. Even if he's evil, there is that little part that isn't, and that part is what makes him himself. It made sense, why would he attend the ball* we held back in Ilimara if he hates it? He was there to distract *me while Aaron killed my Mother.*

I have to get revenge. I will kill Aaron, but first I have to escape. I went back in and heard a knock on my door. I opened it and saw Nathaniel.

"We need to talk," he said and brushed past me. I closed the door, confused.

"What do you have to tell me?"

"They found the Vladium, in two days they'll arrive and then it's your turn," he said hopefully.

"You know what happens as soon as I get my hands on the blade," I said to him. *I really hope this won't even happen. If it does, I'll have to kill myself. Nobody could stop me.*

Pain flashed in his eyes as he remembered what I'd told him earlier. "Please, Astoria, there has to be a way to not kill yourself, I won't let that happen," he said, frustrated.

For a matter of seconds, I thought about telling him about my plan. But I couldn't. *As much as I want to trust him, I can't. He would tell Aaron and I'd be locked up. If he really wanted to help me, he would've run away with me a long time ago. He made his choice.*

"You know there isn't. There is only one option, and I've made my choice," I said and started brushing my hair.

"Why do you sacrifice yourself for those people? You don't even know them, you weren't even in the light realm once!" he said angrily. I can't *believe* he said *that.* Is he really that naïve? I threw my brush onto the desk and turned to face him.

"How can you say that?! These are people, they have a life, they deserve to live!" I yelled.

"You deserve to live too!" he yelled back.

He doesn't *get it,* does he? This isn't *about me!* "I couldn't save my mother, I couldn't save my father, so just let me save someone for once! Let me do the right thing!" I yelled, backing him up against the wall.

"You can save yourself! You don't even know these people!" he yells, his minty breath flooding my nose.

I cannot believe this man! He is a selfish arrogant jerk!

"To you they might be numbers, but they have families, children, parents just because they don't matter to you doesn't mean they don't matter to someone!" I yelled, finally breaking free of whatever was holding me back. "You are a selfish, arrogant jerk who only thinks about yourself! What did I ever see in you?" I asked myself out loud, and chuckled.

"I don't think about myself, I'm thinking about everyone that matters to me!" he reasoned. Of course, he just proved my point.

"And who is that, hm? Your people? Your family?" I taunted him.

"You," he said, and suddenly I was up against the wall, his lips on mine. They were so familiar, yet so unknown. Did I hear that right? Was that another one of his lies? I'm *sure Aaron set this* up so *I* wouldn't *kill myself.* I pushed him away and turned away from him.

"Astoria –"

I interrupted him. "Save it Nathaniel, too much has happened. I can't forgive nor forget what you did," I said, feeling numb. "Leave," I said, pointing to the door. I felt relieved when he left the room, and fell back onto my bed.

It can't go on like this; one second we're making out, the next we're killing each other. That's not how this works.

I can't trust him, I don't think I'll ever be able to trust him again, not after what he did. I tried to push the thought away for a long time, but there was nothing that hurt me more. *He stabbed me the same second he kissed me, how could I ever trust him? This whole situation confuses me. I don't know where we stand, does he care about me, or not?*

Sometimes I feel like I'm the only one that matters to him, but then again *he makes no effort in protecting me from his evil father. If he really cared, he would've helped me escape, no, I wouldn't have ended up here in the* first place. I just wished he did care about me and that he would help me. I still hope that he*'ll change his mind. But of course I know that* won't *happen. He's loyal to his father, he would never betray him.*

I laid myself to sleep, knowing that tomorrow will change everything.

For better, or for worse.

Deal With the Devil

I was standing on the top of a mountain, overlooking the shadow realm. It was peaceful. I could feel someone near me, but no one was there except me.

"Astoria..." I heard a fading voice whisper. It continued to do so until I saw it: the Vladium. It was right there. I turned around to take it into my hands, but just before I was able to touch it, I felt a hand on my shoulder. Startled, I turned around and met a beautiful woman. She looked ethereal, most certainly not mundane.

"My dear, don't run away from it, it'll only make it worse," the woman said. I felt calm in her presence, she radiated peace. She looked beautiful. Her whole body was light blue. Her hair was a beautiful blue, and she wore a robe with jewellery. Just like Nathaniel told me, I thought and suddenly I remembered. She is Sakra, I can't *believe it. I thought she was dead, how can it be?*

"Dear, don't worry about me, listen to what I have to say," she replied to my thoughts. "I came to visit you because I have a message for you. Do not run away into unknown land, protect the Vladium—" she was interrupted as we heard voices coming our way, fast.

These were the hunters from Aaron, I knew their armour, and they were going straight for the Vladium. "Tell me Sakra, what should I do?" I asked her, desperate for advice.

"Don't run away from it like I did, learn from my mistake," she said, and just like that she was gone.

"Don't take it!" I yelled, but nobody heard me. They didn't even see me.

"Astoria!" I heard someone yell in the distance. I woke up and sat bolt upright on my bed, panting. "What happened?" Alyssa asked, worried.

What is happening? Why did I see Sakra, and what did she mean? "I-I don't know," I murmured, trying to calm myself down.

How was that possible, Sakra is dead! Where was I? I had so many questions and she just left me there, all alone. I have to run away, there is no way I will stay here and *help them. Does she want me to die? Nobody can know about what happened. Except Alyssa.*

"Hey, Astoria, talk to me, what is going on?" she asked, both of her hands on my shoulders.

"I-I saw Sakra and she had a message for me."

"And what was her message?" Alyssa asked curiously.

"That I shouldn't run away from it like she did," I said, and buried my face in my palms.

"Maybe she is right, we can't run forever, we just have to find a way to use the blade without destroying a realm," she said, worry clouding her eyes.

"No, I have to go, there's no turning back now. If I don't run now they'll use it tomorrow, no doubt, and there is no way we'll find something before then," I replied.

"What about Nathaniel? He told you everything about Sakra, he could know what it means," she said.

"No, I can't trust him, he can't know of anything and definitely not that I'm escaping," I said.

If he finds out, god knows what'll happen to us, especially Alyssa. It's too much of a risk to ask Nathaniel for help. If my plan works, he'll be unconscious until I'm already out of the city; if my plan fails, I have to kill him. I won't hesitate; he made his choice, so I'm making mine.

"Can we go over the plan again?" Alyssa asked, pulling me out of my thoughts.

"Alright," I took out a map and showed her. "I will attend the ball like normal and do nothing to cause suspicion, then while dancing with Nathaniel I will lead him onto the balcony, out of sight, and then I'll poison him. I will slip into the crowd once again and instead of going to the toilet, I'll go into the gallery, where you'll be waiting, and then we'll take the staff exit and run," I explained while showing her the places on the map, even though she probably knew the castle better than me.

"Are you sure you can poison Nathaniel? What if it doesn't work?" she asked, worried.

"It has to work, and if not I'll have to kill him. Then we'd be even," I said confidently.

In reality I wasn't sure at all, but I had to believe it'll work and Alyssa was already unsure, it would only make it harder. I knew there was only one person who knew how I could betray Nathaniel. I walked through the corridors and came to a stop when I came across the gallery. I stepped into the beautiful room and sat down onto the bench next to her.

"I need your help," I said.

"You're escaping, aren't you?" she asked.

"Raven, you know what they'll do to me better than anyone, I have to try," I exclaimed.

"Why are you telling me this?" she asked, coldblooded. I knew what I had just done, and I had thought this through. We had gotten really close in the last few weeks, and I helped her multiple times.

"So I don't have to kill your brother," I said, copying her behaviour. She turned around quickly, her eyes wide.

"What did you just say?" she asked, almost yelling.

"He won't leave me another choice. That's not what I want either, so I came to ask for help," I explained.

She ran her hand through her red hair which shimmered in the sunlight. "What do you need?" she said, lowering her voice.

"A distraction once I've poisoned Nathaniel," I said. I knew it was the right decision; her brother was her everything. *Even if they don't show it, they care deeply for each other.*

"You said you wouldn't hurt him!" she started accusing me.

"It won't kill him, he'll just be unconscious, and you already have an antidote for it," I explained. "Now, do we have a deal?" I asked, holding out my hand.

She narrowed her eyes, but after some seconds she took my hand and shook it. "Deal," she said, "but I'll keep a close eye on you." Before I went to turn away and go, she took my arm.

"Don't you dare try anything, I'll slice your head off and that would be a shame, you've grown on me," she whispered, and disappeared. I sat down on the bench again and stared at the paintings. One picture could tell a whole story, it was fascinating. I heard someone approach, and when they came closer, I lifted my head to see who it was. Aaron, just *great*.

"Did you know he painted them all by himself?" he asked, walking around the room.

What's he talking about? I thought they were painting*s* that they bought somewhere. "Who painted them?" I asked. Curiosity rose inside of me, I never thought about who painted them. "Nathaniel did," Aaron explained, and looked at the painting next to me.

No way. He is lying, I saw the painting in his room but it is nothing compared to these ones. "I'm not lying, my child, see for yourself," he said and pointed to the edge of the painting. It was his signature, without a doubt.

"He really cares about you, Astoria," he said, and for the first time ever I saw a hint of empathy cross his face.

He doesn't even care about his son, why would he care about anything besides himself? He'll kill me the second after I killed the light realm. "As if you care," I snapped.

"I do, that's why I came here to offer you a place to stay after you do what I told you to," he said, turning towards me.

This is a trick, there is no way he would do that, he'll kill me. He's doing this so I'll do whatever he tells me to.

"Listen, Astoria, Nathaniel had a hard childhood, but since you came here he's been happy, and even if it doesn't look like it, everything I'm doing, I'm doing for my people. You can be my people, too," he said with a little smile on his face.

Did I hear that right? His people? I can't be angry right now, he'll probably lock me up.

"I'll give you time to decide, but I promise you I would let no one harm you in any way. You could live here with Nathaniel and be happy," he said and turned to walk away.

The deal isn't that bad. I like it here, it*'s* grown *on* me, the people are nice, and I could be with Nathaniel. But I can't *trust Aaron,* *he betrayed me once and* he'll *do it again as soon he gets the chance. As much as* I'd *love to take the offer,* I'm *doing this for my people too.*

And my people are not only here, they are everywhere. I've *already made my decision.*

Kiss of Death

The view from the balcony was as beautiful as it always was. Somehow, I'll *miss it here*. *Even if* I'm *held captive,* I still enjoyed the freedom I got. I learned *a lot about the people here,* and the statement that they are bad is wrong. Just because the leader is evil doesn't *mean that all the people are.*

"I told you you'd like it here," I heard a voice state. I didn't bother to look back. "You ready for the ritual tomorrow?" he asked, leaning on the railing next to me.

"As ready as I'll ever be," I replied with the biggest smile. *Jokes on him, I hope he'll feel as bad as I felt when I realised that he betrayed me.* "It is beautiful here, though," I said, letting my gaze wander.

"It was never personal, this whole thing, it has nothing to do with you," he said, and I turned to face him.

"Hm, wait, let me think, how can that not be personal? I'm going to kill thousands of people because of you," I said, as calmly as possible.

"Even if I had feelings for you, which I don't, it wouldn't change a thing. That's how my father is, and he will do anything in order to get what he wants," he said, turning away, looking back over the city.

"He offered me a deal, to live with you in peace after everything goes down," I told him. His head turned in an instant and he stared at me. "I didn't accept, I will kill myself afterwards. You won't have to worry about me," I assured him.

He nodded and avoided my glance. We stood there in silence and after some time I went back in. I heard a murmur come from Nathaniel's mouth, but I couldn't understand it. I didn't bother, and went back to my room. *It's time.* I've waited so long for this moment.

"You ready?" Alyssa asked from the dressing room.

"As ready as I'll ever be," I replied.

She came back with an alluring dress. It was light blue and even had a breast plate "Put it on!" Alyssa said, bursting with happiness.

"It has a cape?", I asked, amazed. The neckline was awfully low, but it made me look like a warrior queen. Everyone would be amazed.

"I chose this dress especially because of the shield, and it's not that big, so you'll be able to run without having to hold the dress up," she said, beaming as I watched her in the mirror. *She thought of* everything, this will work out, *I know it.* "It's a shame you're not allowed to attend the ball with me," I said hugging her.

"We'll see each other as soon as possible," she said, and squeezed a little bit tighter. "And you already have a date, remember?" she said mockingly.

Obviously, I had to attend the ball with Nathaniel. "Don't remind me!" I said, and laid the letter that I wrote earlier on the bed.

I took the knife and put it into the sheath on my thigh. I saw the little bottle on the counter and took it. "How does it work?" I asked Alyssa, and opened the bottle.

"It won't affect you because it'll know that it shouldn't attack you. Once something comes in contact with your lips, it'll be poisoned in a matter of seconds," she explained, and cleaned the rest of my room.

"Alright, now or never," I said, and smeared the poison onto my lips. I felt a little bit lightheaded at first, but after a few seconds I felt pretty normal.

I heard a knock at the door. Nathaniel looked as handsome as ever. His black suit and white shirt stood out, and his hair was different. It was parted in the middle, a little lock on the side of his head. "We look rather dashing today, love," he pointed out.

"I always do," I confirmed, and left the room. We walked next to each other, the corridors filled with tension. Maybe it was my tension; I had to poison him in a few hours.

"What's on your mind, darling?" he asked mockingly.

"You tell me," I mocked him back.

"Let me guess, you're thinking about how you can escape best? The exit won't work, love," he mocked me. My mouth was wide agape, my eyes big. *How on earth did he figure that out?* "It's fine, I read the letter earlier. You're a terrible hider," he provoked me even more. *My plan failed, I failed everyone.* "I won't tell anyone, but I won't let you out of my sight," he said grinning, and we continued to walk.

It's hopeless, I'll never be able to pull this off with him on my heels. At least I tried, it could've worked. I should've never written that letter. Just before we reached the stairs, I took his arm and stopped him.

"Nathaniel, please, you have to let me go," I said looking him in the eyes. They were troubled, something was going on.

"You don't understand, they'll find you and once they do, they won't hold back," he replied. I wanted to scream at him. *I had to try! Even if they would* find me, at least I tried everything I could.

"Astoria," he whispered, lifting my chin up. "Not all hope is lost," he tried to assure me. He was right. *I forgot about the poison, I never wrote that in the letter. It's the one thing he doesn't know of.*

"You're right, it's not over until I say so," I replied, and we took the stairs. I heard several gasps as we walked down into the room.

I spotted Raven in the crowd, and she shot me a little smile. I have to tell her that he knows what's going on. I talked with several people before I went over to the dance floor.

"Here you are," I said to Nathaniel. He leaned on the wall, his head tilted.

"I was busy observing you," he said with a graceful smile.

"That's so thoughtful of you, I never knew you cared about me that much!" I mocked him.

"Of course, you are my most precious possession," he said, full of sarcasm.

"May I have this dance, Astoria?" he said my name differently this time. Genuinely. I took his hand and he led me onto the dance floor. A gentle song was playing, and we quickly found our rhythm together. Our bodies were flush against each other; I could feel his breath on my neck.

"How did you plan to escape, darling?" he whispered.

I can't tell him the truth. I need to find a lie. "Well, I would've gone to the toilet and escaped through the staff exit," I replied, smiling.

"I expected you to lie better than that, you would never plan something that risky," he whispered into my ear, his husky voice making goosebumps run all over my body.

"Well, I expected nothing less from you, spy," I mocked him. "What was it like? Knowing that your own mother died because of you?" I whispered into his ear.

It was time. I didn't know how he would react, but I knew he would be furious. He stiffened, and in one heartbeat he grabbed me.

"Don't ever try to get inside of my head," he snarled. For several beats we stayed there, his grip crushing my wrists. Finally, his eyes softened. "It's too dark for you," he whispered. *Well, I didn't* expect that reaction. I would need another plan.

"I need to get some fresh air, excuse me," I said, and walked out onto the balcony. The quiet was comforting, and I could hear the people talk in murmurs. A cold breeze grazed my skin as I leaned on the railing. The city shimmered with the lights, an ocean full of lights. I felt peace. *I will escape, it doesn't matter how, but I will.*

"The woman of the hour," I heard Nathaniel exclaim as he approached me from behind.

"Astoria..." he whispered, and put a hand on my waist. "Look at me, darling." He turned me around so I was backed up against the railing. "I'm sorry that you think that this is my fault. I did everything in my power to make the time enjoyable," he murmured.

It doesn't change the fact that he stabbed me. He played with me *from* the first time we met. He knew exactly what they would do with me*, and he still went through with it.* I didn't respond. I had nothing left to say to a traitor.

"For god's sake, I love you, that's why I can't let you go, I couldn't bear the thought of you being killed," he whispered against the cold evening breeze. *My ears must have gone crazy, he loves* me?

This is my chance. I can poison him right now, nothing is stopping me.

"That's why I have to do this," I whispered, and put my lips softly on his. It was a light and soft kiss, and a tear escaped my eye as it betrayed everything in me.

I slowly laid him onto the cold ground and checked his pulse.

"Game over," I said, and ran.

Chip

I ran until I wasn't able to breathe anymore. Nobody noticed that I was missing, and Nathaniel was dealt with. When I arrived at the gallery I looked around; there was no sign of Alyssa, and the room was pitch black.

"Alyssa," I whispered, making my way to the exit. That's when I saw her. Hanging from the wall, blade deep in her chest, her body limp. Everything was covered in blood. I felt my blood turn cold as I began to realise what happened. I screamed until nothing came out. I didn't care that they would find me. They should. *I'll kill them all. Every single one of them.*

Suddenly I felt someone pull me out of the way into a hidden corner. My mouth was covered as I tried to scream. I saw the guards standing in front of Alyssa. *She was a good person, she didn't deserve that. This is my fault, I convinced her to escape with me. Without me this would've never happened. It's my fault that she's dead. Just like it's my fault that Mom and Dad are dead.* Soon the guards disappeared, and I tried to get out of the stranger's grip.

"Stop it," I heard an awfully familiar voice whisper.

It can't be. There is no way.

"How?" I asked in disbelief.

"I took the antidote before you kissed me, love. The game is over when I say it is," he whispered and I freed myself from his grip.

"They killed her, Nathaniel! How could you let this happen? She was innocent!" I yelled.

"Keep your voice down and follow me," he said, and looked around before walking away. "Say goodbye, you have half a minute until we have to be gone," he said, and left. I stood in front of her dead body.

"I am so sorry, Alyssa, I broke my promise, I told you I'd keep you safe, this is my fault, I–" My voice broke down as tears started flooding my eyes. "I will never forget your sacrifice. Hail and farewell," I said before leaving.

"Quick, be quiet," Nathaniel whispered softly and took my hand. He led me down the hall and into a small room with nothing in it but a staircase that led into the darkness. "They won't follow, they don't know this room exists, but come on," he said, and he led me into the darkness.

He lit a torch and I slowly looked at my surroundings. We were in a tunnel, and there were spiders and little insects everywhere, disgusting. *Why did he lead me here? Is he helping me?*

No, he's probably making me think that I have a chance, and just before I do it he'll betray me again. What did he mean when he said not all hope is lost? Did he really betray his father? Why would he change his position?

He must've seen the confusion and disbelief on my face, because he was grinning from ear to ear. "I must say, I wouldn't have guessed that you would actually go through with it. You're one brave women, darling," he said mockingly.

"How did you know?" I asked him, mouth still agape.

"Raven told me about your little plan to poison me, I have to say, you should've killed me instead," he replied.

"You're right, I should've, but turns out you aren't evil after all," I stated.

"I'm not doing this for you, love, I'm doing this for myself. He would've killed me if he knew that it was my fault that you ran off," he replied, relaxed.

"I knew you weren't evil," I said, mocking him. By the smile he gave me I knew I was right. I felt relief wash over me knowing that I wasn't alone anymore. "She should have been here too," I whispered, my vision starting to go blurry.

"I am sorry, Astoria, I really am, I didn't know that he did that. It's time something changed in this realm," he whispered and came in for a hug. His scent gave me comfort.

"This is all my fault," I sobbed. *If I would've kept my mouth shut she would still be alive. I convinced her, she doubted and she didn't want to leave, but I made her.*

"No, Astoria, she made her choice herself, the only thing you can do now is to not let her sacrifice go to waste," he assured me. He was right.

I will get my revenge, and once I do I'll kill everyone who is still on Aaron's side.

"Come on, we have to go, as long as we are in this realm they will be able to track you," he exhaled, starting to walk.

"What do you mean?" I asked him. *How would they track me? He is probably lying. No, why would he be lying?*

"There is a chip planted in your forearm, they chipped you when you were unconscious," he explained.

I suddenly felt uncomfortable. God knows what else *they did when I was asleep.* "Take it out," I ordered him. I tried to hand him my blade, but he refused to take it. "Do it, Nathaniel," I commanded him again. I would do it myself, but my left hand is the weaker so I probably wouldn't hit the right spot. He hesitated before taking my blade into his grip.

"On three, one, two—" and he cut through my skin and flesh. I screamed as loud as I could, the pain almost knocking me unconscious. He slowly took the chip out and took a needle and thread out of his pocket.

I don't want to know why he *had those* things with him, *but this will be the painful part.* He started stitching my wound as I gripped onto his shoulder and bit into it. The pain was almost unbearable, though getting stabbed in the chest was worse.

"Alright, let's go," he said, finishing the bandage around my forearm. I started walking, but I stumbled and wanted to sit down again. Nathaniel quickly destroyed the chip, and then he began to carry me. I couldn't keep my eyes open, and when they fluttered I heard him whisper;

"Not all hope is lost."

Waterfall

My eyes flew open as I remembered having the same dream as before: Sakra standing on the mountain, telling me not to run away. *She has to be wrong, I am doing the right thing. I won't* make the same mistake as her, *I won't* kill myself. I still *don't* know why Nathaniel changed his mind. *I'm* glad, *but he shouldn't* have left because of me. *I'm* not sure if I can trust him yet, he might be a spy. This could all be a trick.

"Darling, it's no trick. I'll be killed as soon as they get the chance," he snorted.

I swear sometimes I think he can read my mind. He always knows what I'm thinking about, it's irritating. "For the record, I don't trust you," I said.

His eyes gleamed mischievously, and I knew everything was a game to him. "The feeling is mutual, love," he replied, and continued to walk.

Turns out it was a longer tunnel than I expected. We must have been walking for about four hours now, no doubt. I was beginning to feel tired and let out a yawn.

"We should be almost there, it should be right there," he said, pointing to a ladder. It was gigantic, and I could see the light that came from it. *But where would we end up? What if they are waiting for us just outside?*

"Wait, Nathaniel, what if it's an ambush?" I asked, cautious. He looked back at me I knew that he was worried too.

"We should be in the middle of the forest by now, and it's not patrolled, we should be fine," he tried reassuring me. I took the blade from the sheath just in case. I would be weakened because of my arm, but it should do its job just fine. I went first and started climbing up.

I felt my feet slip, but just as I was about to fall back, I felt strong hands around my waist. "Easy, easy," he whispered, and I continued on. When I was on the ground I saw where we were. Nathaniel was right, we were in the middle of the forest.

It was mysterious. A thick fog blurred my vision, it was cold. "Well, I told you we'd be fine," he exclaimed, pulling himself up as well.

Where do we go now? We *can't* stay in the woods, *it's* way too cold. I *don't* understand. Why would be woods not be patrolled? It would only make sense, you could easily run off and never come back. "Why are the woods not patrolled, Nathaniel?" I asked him, looking around my surroundings with alarm.

"Because there are worse things out here than there are in the city," he said, and I thought I heard a branch crack.

"What do you mean by that?" I asked, eyes wide open.

"They say my father created monsters to make sure no one escaped, and that's why they don't need to patrol the forest," he said, swallowing hard. *Perfect.* Just as I thought everything was over I found out that the worst thing lay ahead of us.

I knew there had to be a catch, but I wouldn't have guessed it was such a big threat. "What kind of creatures are we talking about?" I asked him. The look on his face betrayed his fear. I've *never seen him scared before.* It made me uneasy.

"Ferals," he exhaled. It made sense, I thought I felt something. But the way I felt it, there had to be at least a half dozen ferals in these woods.

"Astoria…" I heard voices scream. "Come and help us," they continued.

"I can hear them, Nathaniel," I gasped, my whole body starting to shake.

"Tell them to visit us, time for some fun," he exclaimed, and took two knives from behind his back. I had no idea that he was armed, but it did make sense. They were coming. I felt them approaching us, at least three of them.

"Remember, don't think about anything, they will use your biggest fear against you!" Nathaniel yelled just before the first one attacked. They were fast. I slashed my knife against one's skin, and black blood sprayed through the air. I took my chance when it stumbled and stabbed the knife right through its heart. The figure was frozen for a few seconds before it let out a horrific scream and evaporated into thin air, disintegrating like ash.

I sensed one of them coming from behind and just before it reached me, I turned around and threw the knife into its heart. I felt heavy breaths escape my mouth as I saw that it was over. Nathaniel smiled with pride as all of them disappeared.

"Well, that was certainly fun," I exclaimed catching my breath. Even though we killed them, I could still feel them around us. There were at least four that we killed. "There are more," I said, and in that exact moment I felt something scratch my back. It attacked fast, and in one swift move it hovered above me. I knew it was about to happen. It'd dig in my head to find something to use against me. And even though I knew it wasn't real, I couldn't help but feel bad when I saw her face.

Her dark chocolate brown face, her raven dark hair. She was innocent. "Astoria, this is your fault, all of it!" she yelled. *This isn't* real. It *isn't*. *It's* all in my head. "It's because of you I am dead now, my blood is on your hands!" she yelled, and when I looked at my hands they were covered in blood. The same blood that was on her face, her clothes, everywhere.

I saw how Aaron drove the blade through her chest and through the wall.

I heard her screaming, she was screaming my name, and I didn't do anything. *Just like when my mother died. I am the problem, everyone around me dies when they need my help. It's my fault.*

I should've never convinced her to come with me, she would still be alive. She would be happy. Instead *she's dead, hanging on the wall. No, this isn't* real. Alyssa would never accuse me of *anything.* This is all in my head.

"You're not real, leave her be!" I yelled, and I sprang up, my eyes twitching.

"Shh Astoria, it was just a hallucination, it was not real," Nathaniel tried comforting me. My breathing was quick and shallow, I was shaking. "Hey, look at me," he said. I was shaking uncontrollably, and he cupped my cheek with his palm.

"It's all my fault," I whispered to myself.

"Astoria," he said loudly, bringing me back to reality. "It was just a hallucination. It was not real, nobody is here, it is not your fault," he tried to convince me.

He was right. *It wasn't* real, it was just in my head. But even if it was in my head, it was true. It is my fault that *she's* dead.

"Everything will be alright," he said, pulling me close.

He's right. It will be alright. It has to be. "We need to leave, right now, they'll come after us and they won't stop," I said, knowing that it was our only option.

"There should be a portal some miles from here, we can start walking, and then we'll be back in the human realm," he explained and picked up his things.

"Alright, let's go," I said, and pushed myself up to my feet.

My muscles ached, and I was beginning to feel exhausted when Nathaniel said, "Come on darling, we're almost there," and finally we were in the middle of a field. The moon shone above our heads, and there were fireflies all over the place; it looked majestic. The portal was blue – you couldn't see into it. I didn't know what to do, so I turned to Nathaniel. He stepped in front of the portal and looked back at me, grinning.

"Are you ready, love?" he asked, offering me his hand.

"As ready as I'll ever be," I replied. I took his hand and we stepped through the portal. We were thrown onto a hard surface. I could tell by the smell of my surroundings that I wasn't in the shadow realm anymore.

For the first time in a very long time, I smelled the scent of nature. It was refreshing. We were in the forest, but this time it looked much more friendly. The trees were greener than they were back in the shadow realm.

"Welcome home," he chuckled, and walked away.

"Where are you going?" I yelled after him, but he was already gone. *Perfect.* I walked after him, trying not to lose his trail.

Suddenly I was at the top of a cliff, overlooking the place I know so well. We were at the waterfall that I had visited with my parents when I was a child.

This time the water shimmered light blue; the only thing that was here as well were the fireflies. It was breathtaking. I took a deep breath and could smell the fresh water. I made my way down to the water, where I saw Nathaniel cleaning himself up from all the blood. He looked like an ancient god. His light hair was still softly parted in the middle.

"It's rude to stare at people when they're cleaning themselves up," he teased. He looked irresistible. I decided to join him in the water and took my dress off. The water wasn't as cold as I had expected, to my surprise. It wasn't deep, it barely covered my chest. The water only covered Nathaniel's legs; he was very tall, at least a head taller than I am. I felt my forearm sting as it collided with the water. It must've healed pretty good, because I barely saw a mark on my arm.

When I approached Nathaniel, I saw blood spreading around his figure. I quickly scanned for where the blood came from. He had a big wound on his stomach. "I'm fine," he exhaled.

"You are not fine!" I yelled. *How could he hide this from me?* "Who did this to you?" I asked angrily.

"My father did, when you tried to run off," he murmured. *No.* "It's just a scratch, nothing to worry about!" he tried convincing me.

"Nathaniel, this is serious! You idiot! Why did you not tell me?" I yelled at him.

"You would think it's your fault when it really isn't, it's my father's fault," he answered.

"No, this is my fault! All of it!" I screamed. *I hurt everyone around me. Nobody is safe.*

"You have to go," I said softly. He didn't react. "Nathaniel, go," I said once again.

"Why would I do that, after everything we went through?" he asked sceptically. He came over and cupped my cheek in his palm, looking down softly into my eyes.

"Because," I stopped letting myself enjoy the moment with him. "Because everyone around me is bound to get hurt or killed, and I don't want that to happen to you," I whispered, a single tear rolling down my cheek.

"Darling, if you haven't noticed already, I'm hard to kill. You're stuck with me, whether you want it or not," he whispered. "Even if it'll kill me, at least I got to be with you until my last breath, and that is enough for a boy like me," he murmured against my lips.

I softly pressed my lips against his. His breath was minty and suddenly I was very warm.

"Astoria," he whispered between heated kisses. Out of nowhere, he doubled over in pain. *I almost forgot about his wound.* It was very deep.

"Let me have a look at it," I said, and we left the water. I told him to lay down, and took the cape of my dress and tore it apart. I took the fabric and tried to bandage the wound with it. He gasped at the sudden pressure I put onto the wound. I couldn't help but notice the anger rising in my chest.

Aaron will pay for this. I'll kill everyone that he cares about. He stabbed his own son! What kind of person does that? We were lucky it wasn't that cold. I laid down next to him and closed my eyes. I couldn't sleep, the images of Alyssa appearing whenever I closed my eyes. The night replayed in my mind.

I felt Nathaniel twitching next to me, his breath quickening. He was shaking, sweat on his forehead. "Please, stop!" he yelled.

Nathaniel was having a nightmare. *What do I do? What do you do when someone has a nightmare? I have* no clue. He continued to scream and shake. I gently shook his shoulders, but he didn't react.

"Nathaniel!" I screamed and shook him again, harder this time. He gasped and I could see that he was confused.

His breath relaxed and he sat up. "Shh Nathaniel, it was just a dream," I whispered and took him into my embrace.

"He-he hurt you," he murmured against my hair. *Nathaniel had a dream about me. I was getting hurt and he freaked out.*

"He can't hurt me, Nathaniel, I'm safe, we're safe," I assured him quietly. He hugged me tighter and let out a deep breath.

"I won't let anyone hurt you ever again," he promised me.

He isn't a monster, they made him into one. I am coming for all the monsters that ever touched him, I am coming for all the ones who twisted his stars into shadows. They turned him into a nightmare, so I'm going to be theirs.

God Save the Queen

We spent a while walking next to each other. I knew the trail, the castle was about two miles away. My whole body was sore, and I needed a real bed. *I hope that Eden is in the castle, I hope he's okay. I feel terrible for letting him be all on his own, ruling a whole kingdom. I had no other choice, but that doesn't make the choice okay. I'm sure he's thriving and enjoying his time. Someone needs to.*

I quietly took Nathaniel's hand, and he gave me a reassuring squeeze. "Nobody will blame you for what happened," he tried convincing me.

"But they will blame you," I continued.

They will kill him. I'm guessing that by now they've discovered that it was Nathaniel who captured me. I need to talk to them before it gets out of hand. He did bad things, but what matters is that he stood next to me when it mattered.

"I can protect myself, darling, don't worry," he said mockingly. *I used to say that, I could've protected myself, but he made it easier for me, so I'll make it easier for him too.* I recognised the familiar streets as we arrived in the city. Nobody was outside, but I saw a storm coming.

That's good, I'm sure they tried to hide the fact that I was abducted. I finally felt like I was safe.

We made our way up the hill. It was hard, walking up, but once you're up, it's beautiful. The castle in all its beauty, the big field next to it, overlooking the sea. I missed it.

"It makes our city look like rubbish," he exhaled next to me as he took a glance. *I would've said it does, but now, after all the time I spent in the shadow realm, I can't help myself but think that it was just as beautiful as it is here. They may be different but both of them have a beauty in them.* It started pouring and I chuckled lightly. *When was the last time I felt the rain touch my skin?* It felt awesome.

I started dancing to a song in my head. A smile started spreading across my whole face, lighting my eyes up. I chuckled at the face Nathaniel made. "Come on, dance with me!" I said, dancing over to him.

"You're crazy, love," he said, but he still started dancing with me. He smiled at me, a genuine smile. I noticed his eyes; they were green instead of grey. When I looked up at him, I could see every constellation, every star in the galaxy. We danced happily in each other's arm until I heard a voice.

"Astoria!" I heard multiple voices call out, running in our direction. As they approached us, I recognised them right away.

Hera was the first to reach me, almost collapsing with me to the ground, Ash threw his arms around me and yelled. "She has returned!" he yelled happily. I missed this dork.

I chuckled lightly and hugged Eden. "I'm glad you're home," he said, relieved.

"Why is this traitor here?" I heard Ash yell at Nathaniel.

"Back off," Nathaniel replied, putting his hands up in defence.

"Tell me Astoria, give me one reason why I shouldn't kill this spy right here, right now?" Ash asked, still facing Nathaniel.

"Because he saved me," I exclaimed hastily, getting between them. *I knew this would happen.*

"He hurt you, we saw the blood!" he yelled. "I swear to god, I'll cut his head off," he said, trying to jump onto him.

"Ash, stop! If you could just listen to me!" I screamed.

In one swift moment Ash was on top of Nathaniel, knife at his throat. *Why can't he just listen to what I have to say? I know he won't listen to me. I can't let him kill Nathaniel, not after everything. If someone's going to kill him, it'll be me.* I hesitated. What should I do?

Without thinking twice, I took my blade and held it at Ash's throat. I heard Hera and Eden gasp behind me. "If you hurt him, I'll kill you," I exclaimed heartlessly.

"Why are you defending this traitor?" he asked sceptically. I could see his knife pressing into Nathaniel throat even harder.

I held my knife even closer to Ash's throat, making sure he felt that I was not kidding.

"Don't you dare do anything, let me explain!" I begged him.

I was telling the truth. If he killed him, I would kill Ash in an instant. I don't know why but I would. He slowly relaxed his grip on his knife. I could see Nathaniel's face, and he wasn't even flinching. He was grinning. *He enjoyed this! He really needs help.*

"Can we handle this like normal people, please?" Hera said, taking Ash's knife.

"Let's go inside, we can discuss it there," Eden commanded.

I heard Ash growl, and I went over to Nathaniel. "This is going to be fun," he mocked me.

"Don't provoke them, don't make it harder than it already is," I begged him. His smile just widened. *I will have to keep a close eye on those two. I can't wait to be home again.*

I missed the light and bright colours, the way everything was kept in place and the sun shone through the windows. We approached the front door, guards were protecting it. They stepped aside and let us pass. When the door opened, my jaw hit the floor.

Everything was dark and destroyed. It smelled horrible, like death was wandering across the halls. "No," I whispered, looking around. Everything was destroyed.

"We tried to rebuild as much as we could, but there is a lot left to do," Eden said behind me.

I could feel someone touch my hand softly; I looked down and saw Nathaniel's hand find mine. He gave it a squeeze.

I can't believe it. I knew it was destroyed, but I never would've imagined that it was this bad.

There was nothing left, everything broken in thousands of pieces. We walked through the broken pieces. Relief washed over me as I saw that the dining room was still the same.

"They only attacked the front side of the building, everything else upstairs should be the same," Eden explained.

A picture of Mom and Dad laid on the counter, both of them smiling. *I hope they are doing okay and that they can be together in peace now.*

"You two, go upstairs and clean yourself up. Meet us for dinner so we can talk," Eden announced.

He was right, I was in need of a shower. "Nathaniel, you can go to one of the guest rooms," I told him, walking up the stairs. Eden was right, everything looked the same. It even looked untouched. I stepped into my room. It looked the exact way I had left it, the dresses still on the floor, even Eden's note he left me on my birthday.

Crazy to think of how things changed. One night can change your whole life and turn it upside down. I took a long bath, but my muscles still felt tense. I saw the sky turning darker by the minute and went into the dressing room.

I took my red velvet dress; it reminded me of the fact that I would be a queen. *I am one.* It complimented my black hair, and I looked alive when I saw my reflection in the mirror.

I swiftly made my way to the dining room. It seemed that I was late. Everyone was already seated, except for me. "You look stunning!" Hera gasped next to me. I saw Nathaniel grin at me. *He had a plan, didn't he? He sat right on the opposite side of the table.*

"You want to enlighten us why there is a traitor sitting at this very table?" Ash grunted angrily. Nathaniel chuckled, which made Ash even angrier.

I kicked him into the shin under the table, making him stop before he could say something wrong. I told them about everything: The Vladium, the shadow realm, and Sakra.

"He was the reason you ended up in this place! How can you be in his presence?" Ash asked, full of disbelief. He was right; it was Nathaniel's fault, and he'll have to live with that his whole life. *I need to convince Ash.*

"What do you guys think about this?" I turned to Hera and Eden.

"It's your decision, Astoria, if you trust him, so do I," she replied. *At least someone was on my side.*

Eden was silent the whole time. Something was off about him. "It's your decision, but I'll keep a close eye on him," he answered tauntingly. The way he talked, there was something wrong. *I can feel it. He can't* even look at me.

"They will arrive tomorrow, what's your strategy?" Eden asked.

What does he mean? Why would they arrive? They don't even know where we are. "They won't, don't worry," I said.

"If you say so," he said, a scowl on his face. I would need to talk to him. *Something is wrong, I know it.* When we finished eating, Hera pulled me aside.

"I need to talk to you, it's important," she said, and led me into a room.

"What is it, Hera?" I asked her.

She looked worried and alert. "It's Eden…" she whispered.

She felt it too. I didn't imagine things. "What about him?" I asked quietly.

"He's not himself anymore, he's obsessed with power, he would do anything for it. I'm sure he's planning something, you need to talk to him," she said, wary of anyone hearing us.

"I'm not sure what it means, but I will," I assured her.

"I really missed you, I'm glad you're back," she said, and hugged me.

"I am too," I replied, and we left the room. Nathaniel and Ash were still sitting at the table. This *won't end well.* I looked over to Hera.

She gave me a nod and I searched for Eden. I searched in his room, but I found nothing. I heard voices from the throne room and slowly approached it, listening to the conversation.

"Tell him they are here," Eden ordered, and the guard left the room, brushing past me. *Who was he talking about?* "Astoria, what are you doing here?" Eden said coldly.

"I came here to talk to my friend," I said, approaching him.

"We were friends," he started, "before you left me alone, with all the responsibility. I had no one!" he yelled, getting angrier by the second.

It was not my fault that I was abducted! I can't believe him, he was the one that left me all alone *at* the academy. "No, you don't get to play this card, you left me alone first!" I yelled back.

There was no hurt in his eyes, just madness. "Do you really think you can just walk in here and play queen?" he yelled furiously. *He wanted that, he begged me to come back.*

162

"Of course, I am the heir to the throne," I exclaimed. *I don't understand, he never wanted the power. What could've possibly changed that?*

"You don't get it, I put us out of our misery, I led my people, I am the king now, I get to decide what happens," he yelled. I saw it. He had gone mad. "That's exactly what happens when you're in power, you always want more; so do I," he said. "Once they arrive tomorrow, you'll have no choice but to see it too," he said, chuckling. There was a letter on the table. I recognised it right away.

It was a letter from the shadow realm. *No, he would never do that. He would never betray me like that, this can't be real. I don't believe this, out of all people, it is Eden.*

"Why?" was the only thing I dared to say.

He laughed, looking at my surprised face in joy. "He promised me more power, he can give me everything I want, I will rule everything!" he said loudly.

He's been manipulated. I *almost feel bad for him.* "He killed Mom and Dad and you help him?! You are just as bad as Aaron!" I yell, getting closer to him.

"I don't care, he was there for me when you weren't, he is not bad," he replied, a serious tone in his voice. It was too late. He was fully convinced. *I won't be able to convince him otherwise.*

There is only one thing I can do. I broke down, sobbing. He came up to me and hugged me. "I am sorry, but I had no other choice," he said softly. *He did have a choice.* I slowly released myself from his embrace, still close to him.

"It's okay, Eden," I caressed his cheek, "but you leave me no choice, either." He never saw it coming.

The blade pierced his chest. I felt tears escaping my eyes; my vision went blurry.

"Forgive me," I repeated to the still air, to Alyssa's soul. "For not avenging you sooner."

A frigid wind swirled around my now kneeling figure, kissing my cheeks and wrapping me up in its embrace.

"God save the queen," it whispered. I felt a heavy weight on my head. Reaching up, I felt the jewels of a crown.

"God save the queen," I whispered back. "And her friend, too."

Confession

I ran to the dining room immediately. *I need to tell them. I still can't* believe it, he betrayed us. I had no choice but to kill him. The real Eden *would've* begged me to kill him. This *wasn't* him anymore, it was a monster that Aaron created. *He'll* pay for this. Eden was my best friend. *He's* everything *I've* ever known. I rushed down the stairs, and they looked up.

"Guys, we have a problem," I said, out of breath. *They look worried; I must look horrible.*

"What's going on?" Hera asked first, standing up to come over to me.

"Where is Eden?" Ash asked, worried.

"Let me guess, my father convinced him to betray us?" Nathaniel said, as if it was the most common thing ever.

"Who's your father?" Ash asked Nathaniel.

"Aaron," we both called out. They stared at us in disbelief. *We can't waste our time arguing about whether they like Nathaniel or not. We need him, I need him.*

"At least we have an advantage; Nathaniel knows everything about them, right?" Hera asked, trying to stay calm.

"Yes, I do, and we have until sunrise to prepare for a fight," he said, coldness in his voice. Ash was sitting down, staring at the ground, still shocked. I kneeled down next to him.

"Listen, Ash, I know this must be hard for you, but I need you now, I can't do this without you. He protected me when you couldn't, I care about you just like I care about him." I tried to calm him down.

"I know, Astoria, and I'm glad that he protected you, but this is personal between me and him. He was my best friend for years and betrayed me as if it was nothing." He stood up and went over to Nathaniel.

Just before I tried to step in between them, Hera held me back. "You have to let them deal this themselves, it's not our place to say anything," she said. She was right. I knew the feeling of someone betraying you.

"Ash, I'm really sorry, I had no other choice but to do it, they would've killed all of you. You're still my best friend, whether you want to be or not. I hope you'll forgive me someday," Nathaniel explained.

I expected Ash to punch him but instead he brought him in for a hug. *This is love. Being able to forgive someone even when they've betrayed you.* I wish I could do it, but I *can't.*

I never felt loved, that's why I stabbed Eden without a second thought. I was used to losing the people close to me; what's one more? Aaron made me kill him to weaken me.

But, just like before, he doesn't know me. I don't get weaker after something like that. I get stronger.

"Hey guys, I'm sorry to interrupt your heartfelt moment, but we don't have much time left," Hera called out, and they turned around. They looked handsome, both of them in suits, their hair perfectly styled.

"We need a strategy." Ash spoke first, looking at Nathaniel questioningly.

"Alright," he said, pointing at the map of Ilimara. "They'll most likely take the same route Astoria and I took. I take it that they are already in this realm, which means we have about until sunrise, like Astoria said," he explained.

"What about weapons?" Hera asked him. "We have a lot of weapons here, but I don't think it'll be enough."

"He'll come alone, no guards. There will be burned ones, just enough to weaken us so he'll be able to strike. Once we're dead he'll take Astoria and use the Vladium," he explained, looking at me.

"But you won't die. We can take out the burned ones with our weapons, then once we have Aaron we'll use our magic," I said confidently. *It's not that hard, we took them out in the forest and now we have two more people, it will be alright.*

"You should stay hidden. He needs you, Astoria; if he doesn't get you, he can't perform the ritual," Nathaniel looked worried. It was new for him to show his emotions. *I like new.*

"No way. I will get my revenge; just like you said, he can't kill me, he needs me," I argued.

"Promise me, Astoria, if anyone gets tortured you won't budge, you will not give him what he needs even if we are in pain," Nathaniel said softly, taking my hand.

He was right, I can't budge, I have to be strong. But he knows me, if any of them get hurt, I'll do everything in my power to help them, nothing would change that.

"I promise." The lie flew from my mouth faster than I thought. "Now go and get some rest. I'll meet you in the morning before sunrise," I said, and they stood up.

"Oh, and Astoria, nobody blames you for what you did to Eden," Ash called out.

I was relieved, hearing that I didn't make the wrong choice. I wished there was another way, but there just wasn't. *I hope he'll forgive me someday.* I felt a warm palm on my shoulder, and I turned to see Nathaniel standing next to me.

"Are you afraid?" he asked. I couldn't figure out if it was worry or coldness in his voice.

"I'm afraid that I'll lose the last people that I care about," I said, without showing a hint of the feeling that I had in that moment. *It's a storm, and I can't escape it.* He caressed my cheek, and I looked up into his green eyes.

"It's alright to be afraid, darling, everyone is," he whispered softly. Truth was, I was terrified; every fibre of my body screamed to not do it. But I had to.

I needed to get revenge for all the people that had to sacrifice themselves for me. *They didn't die for nothing, I have to make sure of that.*

"Hey, it's going to be alright, I promise," he said, looking at me like I was a fragile creature.

"I can't lose you," I said, releasing a deep breath.

After everything we went through, I can't just lose him. Our story just began, it's not done yet. I know he'll survive it, but if we fail he will have to follow his father back, and only god knows what he'll do to him. I won't let that happen. I won't let them make him a monster, because he isn't.

"You will never lose me," he said, and softly pressed his lips to mine. "As much as I'd love to continue what we're doing, we need to rest, love," he said, and we went back into my room.

"So, this was little Astoria's palace," he chuckled, looking around the room.

"Hey! Don't judge. I am the queen, don't make me banish you from my kingdom," I joked.

"Oh, now I'm really scared, your highness," he chuckled. I let out a big yawn and fell onto my bed.

Oh, how much I've missed having a real bed. I looked out of the window above my head and saw the stars wink at me.

I knew I was connected with the stars, but I never felt it. Multiple shooting stars flew across the sky. Nathaniel laid next to me.

"You want to tell me you looked at the stars every night and never discovered that you're connected to them?" he teased me.

"You're right. I was fascinated by the stars since I was a kid, that's why they built a window for me," I said, remembering the debate. They told me it was unnecessary, but I insisted on getting a window. It was the best decision. I found myself getting lost in the stars almost every night, fascinated by their beauty.

"Did you know…" he stopped. I turned over to look him in the eyes, the stars reflected in them. "…when I look into your eyes, I see the stars? Your eye colour changes when you see someone you love. That's why I always knew you loved me." He let out a light chuckle. His dimples appeared, and it made him look even cuter. That*'s* why his eye colour changed!

"Yours changed too, they've been dark green for some time now, but I never told you," I whispered. *He loves me. He does care.*

"That's one hell of a love confession," he laughed.

"Even though we never said it to each other, we always knew, didn't we?" I asked.

He didn't need to tell me that he cared about me.

His actions showed me that he did, even though his words never matched his actions. Actions speak louder than words.

"Do you want to know when your eye colour changed?" he asked softly.

I'm guessing since he changed his mind and helped me escape. I nodded slightly.

"When you poisoned me at the ball, your eyes changed. That's why I was so confused," he murmured. *I had no idea. The hurt I felt that night must've made me realise that I do care about him a lot.*

For the first time in a while, I closed my eyes knowing I'm safe and right where I'm meant to be.

I was on a battlefield, and I could see myself. I could observe the situation. Everyone was there; I had the Vladium in my hand. I felt someone put a hand on my shoulder. I saw Sakra, floating in the air next to me.

"My dear, do not make the same mistake that I did. Don't kill yourself," she said. *She tried to warn me not to run away, she was right.* "The light and shadow realm were once one. You always have a choice, never forget," she said, and disappeared.

I sprung up, sweat on my forehead. *What was that? What did she mean? They were once one. What is it supposed to mean?* I felt so confused, thousands of thoughts crossing my mind.

"Sakra, guide me," I muttered into the air around me.

"You already have it in you, you know what it means," I heard her say in my mind.

They were once one.

Oh!

I know what I have to do.

The question is, am I willing to do what it takes?

Eye for an Eye

It was dark when I stepped out onto the balcony; it reminded me of the castle in the shadow realm. They *were* similar in a way. I saw the sun slowly appearing on the horizon and I knew it was time. I strode over to my closet and took the armour out. It was embellished black leather which fit tight around my waist. I looked like I was ready for a war.

I went to the weapons room and took multiple blades and a bow out of it. I put it over my shoulder and made my way to the dining room.

Nothing would be the same after tonight. He swore he would come back for me, and I was ready to destroy him. *He took everything from me, and I am ready to do the same. I overcame everything he has thrown at me and came back stronger.* I walked down the marble stairs, thinking of every loss I had suffered, and I could feel the power surrounding me.

He doesn't know who he's dealing with. I am Astoria, the Queen of Ilimara.

I saw all of them standing there, prepared. We were really doing this.

Hera's armour complemented her light hair; she looked gorgeous. Ash had a green cape, which resembled his green magic. Nathaniel also had his armour on, his hair was all over the place, and his blade was at his waist. I heard a loud screech outside. They were here.

"He's expecting a fight," Ash said, confident.

"He wants a fight? I'll bring him a war," I said and walked out, seeing Nathaniel smile proudly at me.

"Whatever happens…" I yell over my shoulder, "…ad astra per aspera," I said.

"To the stars through difficulties," Nathaniel translated, and we stepped outside. It was silent; nobody was there.

"It's a trap," I said, carefully making my way to the field next to the castle. I put on my cape and that's when I saw it. The burned ones were flying directly at us at immeasurable speed.

"Let's have some fun," I heard one of them call out as they attacked. I quickly took my bow and shot at one of them. It gave a loud scream and evaporated mid-air. The others were busy fighting with them, but we wouldn't be able to fight all of them one-on-one.

"Guys, give me cover and I'll shoot them from the sky!" I yell and they started covering me. I shot many arrows, and all of them hit. Thank god for the training I had as a little kid.

They were starting to attack us from all sides. I tried my best to shoot them, but it wasn't enough. The others had to back up, and I saw Hera fighting two at once. One of them evaporated, and she was so busy fighting the other that she didn't notice another one coming from behind.

"Look out!" I yelled, and slashed one of my blades through its chest.

"Thanks," Hera said, breathing hard. Nathaniel killed each one in one swift moment, and together with Ash they were stronger than ever.

I felt him. He was here.

"Are you such a coward? Come out and fight me!" I yelled, and it began pouring rain.

"Well, Well, Well," I heard him bellow, walking towards us, "if it isn't my favourite queen," he jeered. There was still a distance between us. "Emorea!" he yelled, and the burned ones all evaporated in seconds.

"Hello, son," he said, looking at Nathaniel. Nathaniel avoided his gaze, and looked at me instead. "I see where your loyalties lie, you always were a coward," Aaron snorted.

"Astoria," he started, smiling, "I'm going to give you a choice here. Either you give me my son back, or I'll kill him, right here, right now," he called out.

He wouldn't kill his own son, I know it. He's just using it to give him time. But to do what? "Nathaniel, don't you dare go near this monster!" I commanded.

"Then I'll make him come to me," Aaron scowled, and threw a spear at me. It grazed my leg just enough to make it bleed. I gasped, and in the same moment I heard Aaron call out to Nathaniel.

"Either you come with me, or your little girlfriend will be in much more pain. I might not be able to kill her, but I can make her wish she were dead," he taunted.

No, he can't go with him. "Nathaniel, remember what we promised each other?" I yelled in pain. *I won't let him go.*

"Leave her alone!" Hera yelled, throwing her magic at him. He didn't even flinch; instead, he smiled.

"Freeze," he commanded, and suddenly neither Hera nor Ash could move. I saw the terror in their eyes. He threw another spear, and it grazed my side. I wasn't able to move before it hit me, and I screamed as I felt the hot pain run through my whole body.

"Choose," Aaron yelled, threatening to throw another one.

Nathaniel threw me a sideways glance. "I'm sorry, you promised, I didn't," he mouthed, and stepped forward.

"Okay, okay," Nathaniel called out, soothing Aaron, "I'm coming," he said and stood at Aaron's side.

No! I won't let that happen. I *can't* let that happen. I stood up, despite the pain I felt, and walked closer to them.

"Use the Vladium," Aaron said to me, threatening me.

I can't, I won't do it. I will not destroy a whole realm. I *can't* kill more innocent people. I didn't move. He put Nathaniel on his knees and held the knife at his own son's throat. I tried not to scream or move. The Vladium was there, to the side, it was calling my name. *Sakra* was calling my name.

"Use the Vladium, Astoria," Aaron repeated once again. Ash and Hera tried moving, but they couldn't. There was no way we could win this war.

"All hope is lost," I whispered in defeat.

The voice in my head suddenly rang out once more. "You always have a choice, always," it called. *They were once one. A* memory arose in my head. I didn't know what it was, but I made my way to the Vladium. It was glowing with power as I came near it. I looked over my shoulder at Nathaniel. His eyes begged me not to do it. *I don't want to do it.*

I picked the blade up, and the sky rumbled. The bright light shone from the blade as I raised it into the air. I didn't know what I should do. I had no clue what I *was* doing. Why was I holding the blade?

Aaron was fascinated by the momentum that he just witnessed. "Now Astoria, say the words: in absentia lucis, tenebrae vincunt," he yelled. *I could stop, he* would never kill his own son.

They were once one, I remembered. I wouldn't make the same mistake Sakra did. I didn't know why, but somehow, I knew the exact words I had to say. I held the blade high over my head.

"Omnia iam flent quae posse negabam!" I screamed, and drove the blade into the ground beneath me.

"No!" I heard Aaron scream.

"Thank you, Astoria, for bringing both of the realms together again," I heard Sakra whisper in my head.

I did it. I won. I combined the two realms; they will have peace again. I can't believe I actually did it.

I saw Nathaniel smile at me gratefully as he watched me. I felt a wave of anger rise inside of me, images of the people Aaron killed, people I had to kill because of him.

"And now for you," I growled, approaching them. *He killed everyone I ever cared about. I will kill him. I won't have mercy, I have no mercy left for him.*

My eyes found Nathaniel's as I saw pure peace in them, his eyes shining the most beautiful green I've ever seen.

"You! You destroyed everything I worked for my whole life!" he yelled at me, his grip tightening on the blade at Nathaniel's throat.

He wouldn't do it. He's his son. No parent, evil as they may be, would ever sacrifice their children.

"Nobody else's blood must be shed today," I said, cautious.

"That's where you're wrong, my child. An eye for an eye," he said and slit Nathaniel's throat in one swift motion.

I fell to my knees and held him as he crumpled onto the ground. I didn't care about anything but him. His eyes locked with mine, as I saw only one thing in them: endless love and peace.

"May we meet again," he whispered with his last breath. I held him close as I saw his green eyes turn grey. I screamed, crying uncontrollably. *I can't lose him. I lost so many people. I can't lose him too.*

"Hail and farewell," I heard Aaron mutter under his breath, standing over us with grief in his eyes.

He has no right to grieve his death. It was his fault. He killed him. He killed the one thing I had left. I felt the anger consume me, taking control over my body.

"You!" I screamed, but my voice sounded different. I felt the power consume me, floating around me, ready to be used. Aaron looked terrified. He stumbled back.

"When they said an angel and a devil fell in love once, and it didn't end well, I didn't believe them. I should've," he said, horrified.

I didn't care what he said, the power burned at my fingertips, it burned my whole body. "An eye for an eye," I said, and threw my power at him at full speed. He fell back and screamed in pain.

"Be glad that your fate is decided by the gods and not me! Pray that they'll have mercy on you, because I don't!" I said, and threw my magic once again. It hit him right in the chest, and as he evaporated into thin air all I could hear was his tortured screams, echoing through the cold air.

Hera and Ash were released and came rushing over to me. "Astoria!" Hera yelled, hugging me. I felt numb. They were happy, congratulating me.

We won, but at what cost? I thought, looking down at the lifeless body of Nathaniel.

Resuscitation

I never should've convinced them to help me. I knew I would hurt some-one, I always do. Everyone around me eventually dies because of me. I refuse to believe that Nathaniel is dead. Just like that. How can one person's life be over just like that? Why do we have that much power over other people? This is my fault, everything that happened. I thought killing Aaron would make me happy, but I was wrong. All I wanted was peace. For once in my life to feel the absolute bliss of peace. Was it that much to ask for?

I snapped out of my thoughts when I heard Hera and Ash softly crying. "Can you guys give me a moment?" I asked them quietly. *I need to be alone with him.*

"Of course, take your time. We'll be waiting for you," Hera said, taking Ash by the arm and disappearing. I was still kneeling over his still body.

"I'm sorry I couldn't protect you, I can't believe you're gone. I don't think I'll ever recover from this; even though I hated you with every fibre of my body, I still loved you more than anything in the world. I wish I could've showed you that a little more, I wish I could've held you one more time. Maybe it was meant to be like that; you always said we'd be the death of each other. How can I make this right? There has to be a way of fixing this. I just have to find it," I whispered to his dead body.

I caressed his cheek, it was cold. "You can't leave me here, I can't do this alone—" my sobs interrupted me as I broke down. I bent over the dead body, holding him tight in my embrace. "You brought me back to life again, I have to do this for you too. There has to be a way, I know it. Please, let me make something right once in my life. I can't lose you too, I need to do something that is right. I am done with making the wrong choices at the cost of others, it sucks," I said, breathing hard.

I felt the emptiness in my heart, like there was a big gap. It physically hurt me. I was in so much pain. *Why does this keep happening to me? Why does everyone around me die? Am I poisonous? I am a danger for everyone. Maybe Sakra's fate was mine after all. I would be doing something good for everyone if I was* be gone. They could live happ*ily and without danger.*

I picked the Vladium up and held it to my chest. My fight was over for good. *This is what's best for everyone. I should've done this a long time ago.* I pressed the tip of the blade harder against my chest, but then I heard a high tone ring. I felt a presence; vibrations went through my whole body. I knew I had felt this before, right when I passed away and Angel Azrael came to get me.

Wait.

I looked down at my chest, and the tip of the blade was still hovering above my skin. *He isn't here for me. He's here for Nathaniel. But why can I see him?* For the first time in a while, I felt peaceful. His presence made all my worries go away – except one. Nathaniel.

"Oh, well, hello there, Astoria," he said, hovering above us.

"H-hello," I said. I was shy, his presence impressed me. *There is something about him, I can't tell what it is, probably because he's an angel. What did Aaron say? I am the child of an angel and demon? Could it be? No, there is absolutely no way, he just wanted to mess with me. I won't let him haunt me.*

"You know why I am here. I must say, I've been a busy man since I last saw you," he chuckled.

Because of me. He was busy because so many people died because of me. "I'm sorry, I never meant for any of this to happen," I said in my defence. He just laughed.

"I know, my dear, I know," he said still chuckling.

"But why can I see you?" I asked him curiously. *I shouldn't be able to see him, he is the angel of death. You can see him once you're dead. Am I dead?*

"Don't overthink it, my dear, you can see me because we have already met. You know, it's not common for people to die and come back, only to see me again," he said, amused.

He was right. I was everything but common. *I know not all hope is lost for Nathaniel. It can't be over for him. This isn't how our story ends.* "Is there something I can do for him? So that he'll come back to life?" I asked pleadingly.

"I do not think we should do that," he answered.

"Why? What would stop me from bringing back someone I care for?" I yelled. I was angry, *why* can't he just help me?

"There are consequences that are far more terrible to live with," he finally replied. *I don't care about damn consequences. I want him back. I would do anything to get him back. Anything.*

"Please help him, I beg you!" I screamed at him, knowing he was the only thing that could help him.

"I do not carry the power to do so," he exclaimed. I knew he was lying. I read it all the time, people brought back to life.

«How come when mortals want things, their only option is to make a deal with hell and sell their soul? Why can't they make deals with God in exchange for good behaviour?" I asked him in disbelief. He considered his answer for several seconds.

"Humans make those deals all the time," he said finally, "they just don't make them with God."

"Then who are they making them with?" I asked.

"Themselves," he replied.

I don't understand. I don't have to understand. The only thing I want is to bring Nathaniel back. "Please," I begged him, now crying. *This is my only chance at bringing him back. After that all hope is lost.*

"There will be consequences, but I'll do it for you, my dear," he said comfortingly. He knelt down next to Nathaniel and looked up at me.

"We won't see each other for a while, but know this, I'm always watching over you and protecting you from the dangers that are out there," he said with pure joy in his eyes, maybe even tears. He evaporated into thin air before I could ask him what he meant. He was gone, and everything was silent.

I watched him closely, praying that it worked. Nothing happened. "Please," I repeated, over and over again. I saw his chest expand and felt relief wash over me.

"Nathaniel," I whispered, turning his head in my direction. His eyes slowly opened. He stared at me, confused. Suddenly he sat up next to me in disbelief.

"I-I was dead, I saw it, why am I here? What is happening?" he asked, confused. He looked horrified.

It felt comforting, seeing him breathe and move. "Shh, everything is fine, you're home," I whispered, cupping his cheek.

He looked at me as if I was a complete stranger. His eyes were distant; I noticed the colour. Grey.

Was this what Angel Azrael meant? The consequences?

"Astoria?" he asked and when I looked at him his eyes turned green.

I flung my arms around him, holding him close. "Don't you dare leave me ever again," I said, laughing.

"I'm not planning to," he replied.

Nothing could destroy this moment. Everything we did, lead to this exact moment. I am so utterly happy.

"I love you, Nathaniel," I said, and this time it was serious. In the corner of my eye, I could see the stars align.

"I love you, too, Astoria," he said, and kissed me.

Oh, how much I missed him. I thought I had lost him forever. And that's when I realised.

We *will* be the death of each other, because if one dies, the other will too.

Strangers

Flash forward 6 months...

I ran away from him, giggling. "I'll get you!" he yelled, chasing after me. I ran as fast as I could; I was panting and out of breath. I felt him getting closer, and I decided to give up. He caught me by my waist, preventing me from escaping.

"You're one fast women, I'll give you that," he said, out of breath. I was smiling gracefully at him, his green eyes sparkling in the afternoon sun. He was beautiful. He let out a laugh and hugged me. His face nestled into my hair, I held him close, taking in his familiar scent.

I am so utterly consumed by our love. I am finally happy. He is my happy place. I would endure all the pain I went through again in a heartbeat, if it meant that I got to know him.

We were on the big field, near the academy. We spent most of our time here together. It became our place. Ash and Hera joked about us getting married; they were happy, and we spent a lot of time with them. After the battle with Aaron, I was named a hero.

Turns out I really did bring both of the realms back together. And they did not fight each other, they lived in peace, families reunited.

Everything turned out to be alright in the end, but this isn't the end. Even if it were, I would be okay, because I have everything I need right by my side.

"What does it feel like being the biggest hero in history?" he joked.

I couldn't help but smile at the thought. "Asks the person who came back from the dead," I replied sarcastically.

They would tell our stories to the children of future generations. I am still the Queen of Ilimara, but I was able to find a way to still attend the academy. "We gave them the story of the century," I said, smiling at myself. *We actually did it.*

"I expected nothing less, darling," he said softly, looking me in the eyes. There was one thing that bothered me. I had a strong desire to know where I was actually from. After Aaron told me that I was the child of an angel and a demon, I couldn't help but feel intrigued. *Could it be possible?* I had a feeling that I met Angel Azrael because of a reason. Not only because I was dead, because I am his daughter. He did tell me he would always watch over me. I hope I'll get my answers soon.

He did lie though, there were no consequences for Nathaniel. He was fine, as if nothing ever happened.

We can finally live happily ever after. Not a day passed where I didn't think about Mom, Dad and Alyssa. I know that they are not gone; they will be in my heart forever.

All of them have a special place. My thoughts slipped away when Nathaniel ran off, a grin on his face.

"Catch me if you can," he yelled, running away. *Here we go again.*

"You bet I will," I replied, starting off. I giggled and laughed and almost had to stop. I was beaming with happiness and joy. I hadn't felt that happy in years.

I came to a stop as he stopped running. We were both chuckling and out of breath. That's when I saw where we were. The breeze of the ocean underneath us brushed against my skin softly. I smelled the fresh salty air around us. The sun began to set, giving us an amazing view. I let my eyes wander around the beautiful landscape.

I looked over to Nathaniel, only to see him watching me. His eyes were glistening; was he crying? The smile on his face told another story. He smiled at me with his gorgeous smile, his dimples showing. I couldn't help but be amazed. He stepped closer to me, holding my waist gently. He put his forehead against mine, a tear escaped his eyes as he smiled.

"Forgive me," he whispered and gently kissed me. I had no thoughts.

I was in my mind. Nathaniel held my hand tightly as the memories arose. As I made my way over to the bar, I suddenly felt someone bump into me. I almost fell, but the stranger caught me with his hands on my waist. I looked up into grey eyes, staring at me.

"I'm sorry for bumping into you, are you alright?" I asked the handsome stranger.

"You were quite lucky, that fall could've torn your dress easily," he smirked.

His ginger hair shone in the light from the chandelier, and I couldn't get past the thought that I must have seen him before; there was an instant connection.

"Do I know you by any chance?"

"We'll meet again soon, Astoria," he said. I saw Nathaniel softly turn into air as the memory disappeared.

When I looked over, I saw him standing next to me, still holding my hand. Another memory came flooding back in an instant.

Most of them were average looking boys, the ones that you'd expect to be here, but one in particular caught my eye. I would recognise his grey eyes anywhere, as well as his ginger hair, perfectly parted in the middle, making his hair fall to each side.

"You're the one I bumped into at the ball! What a coincidence meeting you here," I said happily.

The first time we truly met each other. I couldn't help but smile as I saw him disappearing into the shadows.

Suddenly I was in the corridor of the academy. I felt terrible and my chest was hurting, I felt someone carrying me gently as I murmured something. I heard two people arguing, but I was too tired to catch what it was about.

"What did you do to her Nathaniel?" I heard Ash call out.

"Just help me get her to her dorm," Nathaniel said hastily.

"Not before you tell me what's going on and if she's alright," Ash said, even more pissed off.

"Look man, either help me or get out of my way, she needs to rest," Nathaniel gave back. "I didn't mean to hurt..." was the last thing I could hear before blacking out again.

The memory hurt me to think about, he was so overwhelmed. I saw him turn into ash as I watched the memory.

Another memory appeared. "Already tired of me I see," he said with an amused voice.

"Can you blame me?" I said with an attitude I didn't knew I had.

"Well, I certainly like a challenge, don't you?" he said.

"Oh you're on, but I swear if you even think of distracting me I'll chop your head off," I said, and almost couldn't hide my smile.

"The feeling's mutual," he said, leaning over. Our first class together; if only we knew how far we'd come.

Wait, why was I there? He dissolved into ash once again.

"Astoria, there is nothing missing from you. You, and you alone, are the only thing you need, everything else is irrelevant. Believe me, it'll fade away slowly, if you let it," he said his hand lingering on my cheek as my tears fell.

I felt sleepy and I only heard snippets of what he said, I rested my head on his lap as he stroked my hair.

"Tell me a story," I murmured. And so he did…

I can't remember why I was there, I just remember the memory. But why was I that sad? I don't understand. He slowly started fading away.

I didn't have time to think about it; a new image already appeared.

"Even if you never met your mother, I see her in you, the kindness, it's there, I saw it," I assured him wiping his hair out of his face.

"But you still won't be able to forgive me, ever?" he asked, insecure.

Why would Nathaniel ask me that? I threw a questioning look over my shoulder. Nathaniel just smiled and gave my hand a squeeze. He evaporated into thin air.

"That's why I have to do this," I whispered, and put my lips softly on his. It was a light and soft kiss, and a tear escaped my eye as it betrayed everything in me.

I slowly laid him onto the cold ground and checked his pulse.

"Game over," I said, and ran.

I can only remember snippets from that night. I was escaping, but why would I run away from him?

"Did you know…" he stopped. I turned over to look him in the eyes, the stars reflected in them. "…when I look into your eyes, I see the stars? Your eye colour changes when you see someone you love. That's why I always knew you loved me." He let out a light chuckle.

I can't remember that happening. This must be a mistake, these are not my memories. He slowly turned into air once again.

The last memory appeared before me.

"Nathaniel," I whispered, turning his head in my direction. His eyes slowly opened. He stared at me, confused. Suddenly he sat up next to me in disbelief.

"I-I was dead, I saw it, why am I here? What is happening?" he asked, confused. He looked horrified.

It felt comforting, seeing him breathe and move. "Shh, everything is fine, you're home," I whispered, cupping his cheek.

He looked at me as if I was a complete stranger. His eyes were distant; I noticed the colour. Grey.

Was this what Angel Azrael meant? The consequences?

"Astoria?" he asked and when I looked at him his eyes turned green.

I flung my arms around him, holding him close. "Don't you dare leave me ever again," I said, laughing.

"I'm not planning to," he replied.

Nothing could destroy this moment. Everything we did, lead to this exact moment. I am so utterly happy.

"I love you, Nathaniel," I said, and this time it was serious. In the corner of my eye, I could see the stars align.

"I love you, too, Astoria," he said, and kissed me.

The memory stood still; Nathaniel evaporated into thin air on the image. I let out a gasp, *this is not happening.* I opened my mouth but it was already too late.

The consequences that Angel Azrael mentioned were to forget Nathaniel and everything we had.

And when I looked over as the memory disappeared, I saw a stranger holding my hand.

"Who are you?" I asked the unknown person in confusion.

"May we meet again," he muttered, before slowly dissolving into thin air.

Happy Endings are Overrated

… And they are strangers again.

Dear Astoria, *6 months after*
So here we are after all this time. You're there & I'm here. I could have sworn that it was never meant to go like this. For some reason when I was with you, I completely forgot about the world. I forgot about time and the fact that things change. I was so head over heels for you, that I forgot that this wasn't a fairy tale, and that we don't always get happy endings. You said I'd see you tomorrow, but I guess tomorrow never came. Because here we are, you there, and me here.

1 year after
But my worst fear of all, is that I will have to remember you longer than I got to know you. That I will retain this beautifully lonely memory of you, while you are existing somewhere else, with another. And that soon, I won't really know you at all.

18 months after
I think it's time I let you go. And that's so hard to do, because some part of me will be in love with you for the rest of my life. But the daydreaming, the running in place, it's not healthy. So, this is me, cutting the cord. This is me doing what I should've done years ago. I've been stuck on the same chapter for a while now, unable to turn the page. Focusing too much on things said and done. Reliving every moment, wishing things could have been different. But I can't go back, and if I stay here too long, I won't get to read my happy ending. I think it's time to write a new chapter. May we meet again, love.

And he hadn't left her forever. He watched her every day, every night, always. And one night he looked from the stars as she was looking at the sky, and for a brief moment they looked each other in the eye. And for a moment heaven and earth were connected.

Back to the stars.

Perhaps I'll find you there.

I would like to gratefully thank my best friend, Cecilia, who's beared to stay by my side through all the tears that have been shed in the making of this book.

Furthermore I'd like to thank my English Teacher Mister Hoch for helping me be the writer I am now and never giving up on me.

The author

Lina Fischer is a 15-year-old student from Zurich
who has enjoyed writing ever since she became
an avid reader. Having spent time on exchange to
the United States of America, Lina enjoys travel,
as well as skiing, and has skill in playing the piano
and diplomacy. The Falling of the Stars is her debut
novel.